Written on a Stranger's Map

ROGER KING

GRAFTON BOOKS
A Division of the Collins Publishing Group

LONDON GLASGOW
TORONTO SYDNEY AUCKLAND

Grafton Books
A Division of the Collins Publishing Group
8 Grafton Street, London W1X 3LA

Published by Grafton Books 1987

British Library Cataloguing in Publication Data

King, Roger
Written on a stranger's map.
I. Title
823'.914[F]   PR6061.I473

ISBN 0-246-13163-2

Printed and bound in Great Britain by
Robert Hartnoll (1985), Bodmin
Photoset in Linotron Electra by
Rowland Phototypesetting Ltd
Bury St Edmunds, Suffolk

To my parents

PART I

1

He had always said that when he no longer had the interest to marvel at the grand piles of clouds seen from an aeroplane window, or to imagine how it might be to fall through them into the clear air below, or to wonder why the lines of breaking surf did not move towards the shore, or who it was, exactly, emerging from a hut into a forest clearing at first light, he had always said that when he would rather read the in-flight magazine, he would know that he was lost.

Fuller stared through the window of the DC8 seeing nothing, the caution of his younger self only grazing his mind. The magazine lay discarded on a vacant seat. From the seatbelt sign and their nearness to the ground he guessed it was Kangaba, that the city on the coast was Kingston. There was no attempt to approach an airport, the pilot seemed lost or intoxicated, forcing the elderly passenger plane to make wing-tip pirouettes above the hills then swoop low over the city and out across the sea. The sea glittered too bright, too pretty. Fuller, his large body wedged more firmly in its window seat by the violent forces, was unimpressed, his gaze unmoved. The air outside would be hot, the situation difficult. Inside, drops of condensation sprinted across the plastic trim and spotted Fuller's shirt.

As if angered by his impassivity the plane made a lower and more dangerous pass above the docks, forcing an intimacy with obsolete derricks and a few old coasters, before dashing on across the bay to skim the mangrove swamps. Fuller pressed the plastic cup of whisky to his paunch, weary at this fresh conceit: the port merely a wound, the country its infection.

In Paris, between the flight from Thailand and the one to West Africa, Hugh Fuller, fifty-one, had phoned his wife in Newbury. Sheila said everything was OK in Newbury, Andrew and Melissa were fine. No, there hadn't been any more trouble with the roof. Fuller had explained that the job in Bangladesh had overrun and the Bank seemed to think the Kangaba mission was urgent, so he wouldn't be home for a month or two. She had laughed a bit and said, 'What's new?' and 'We'll expect you when we see you.' He had wanted to say something affectionate and sentimental but he thought that after all these years it was not fair, and that she might not respond.

In Mauritania the plane had made an unscheduled stop and thirty muscled Frenchmen in casual clothes walked away from it towards Sahara sand-dunes, a single building and eleven fighter planes in desert colours. The French were fighting a small unreported war. Fuller had tried to keep this knowledge from himself. Since Senegal the forest had been seamless, giving no clues to the borders of countries.

Seven miles above Morocco he had tried to read the Briefing Sheet on Kangaba but stumbled on the statistics. On the back Schwartz in Washington had handwritten a note in Pentel fibre-tip:

Hugh, you're probably getting the picture that Kangaba is another international basket-case. Government corruption is a fact of life and the President has a hand in this and most other things. There's not much point at the moment in coming to any agreements that do not have his support. What we need here, Hugh, is for you to identify the economic and political pressure points. We've got a sick patient on our hands and some sort of surgery is inevitable. I'm sure you'll sort out what's what before the heavy mob arrive for the December aid donors' meeting. They tell me the people are charming. Look forward to seeing you in DC before too long. Regards to Sheila.   Ted.

Fuller had grimaced as if he had tears to hold back, which he did not.

The horizon dropped from view facing him with scattered clouds, a pale morning sun and blue and blue, then as the pilot switched direction it rushed past again like a flood-tide waterline to be lost to the intimate detail of individual trees, the pattern of rust on slum house roofs, washing in yards. His eyes stayed blank, resisting all that was pressed on them.

Recently, in Manila, Fuller had met a man who knew his wife. He told Fuller that she had told him that she had more money than she needed. She had joked that she would give Fuller's earnings to charity to make up for her husband. The plastic glass cracked in Fuller's fist but he continued to stare through the window. It had never occurred to him that the money was not needed.

The plane made another pass and this time, seeming to weary of its efforts, it found a line of bared earth among the trees, which led to grass, which led in turn to rows of runway lights blinking in the daylight as if surprised at their own illumination. They made a perfect landing and the trees of Kangaba were around him.

2

According to the Briefing Sheet there were in Kangaba four point seven million souls. According to the Briefing Sheet they each earned per year a hundred and twenty-seven dollars, US, and lived, four-fifths of them, in rural places. This is what Fuller had learned, the nausea rising. According to the Briefing Sheet the Kangabans exported iron and in return got oil and rice and manufactured goods. Each year the population grew by two point seven per cent. The situation in Kangaba was, according to the Briefing Sheet, critical, their exports not enough to pay their debts to foreign bankers.

At the bottom of the Briefing Sheet, to where Fuller's eyes had plummeted, there were listed Human Factors, which, according to the Briefing Sheet, were thirty tribes, the Mandinka and the Fula dominant, three religions, Christian, Moslem, traditional – not ordered by importance – and, in Kingston, the élite descendants of ex-slaves. Fuller had dropped the Briefing Sheet, which looked like any other, and waved away the stewardess who came to collect his plastic glass of whisky.

3

Across the hotel lounge a girl on her own was eating a hamburger very slowly. She leaned on her elbows, held the hamburger in both hands and tugged with her teeth to break a piece away. All the while she kept her eyes on Fuller.

'She wants you to pay for the hamburger,' said the barman.

Fuller turned to him but not for long enough to accept a conspiracy. By the time he turned back she had pushed the plate away and a pink tongue was cleaning her lips of crumbs. He beckoned and in response she brought a slow index finger to her chest. He nodded.

'What's your name?'

'They call me Regina.'

'Regina?'

She nodded.

'I'm Hugh.'

'She's just one of the girls who hang around hotels,' said the barman.

Instead of protesting she dropped her head to her chest, showing Fuller a ball of tight black curls.

'Is she a bad girl?' He tried a light tone but the barman shrugged and looked away as if the question had no meaning and, anyway, his interest had only been a passing one.

In his room Regina first sat on the bed with her hands pressed down between her knees, then she got up and leaned this way and that in front of the mirror. All without speaking.

'Would you like a bath?'

She looked at him, walked to the bathroom and looked at the bath. She turned on the tap and water trickled from the shower on to her head, surprising her. Now she smiled. She was pretty.

Fuller left her, showing trust. He lay on the bed and wondered whether he could still send her away, whether she would cause trouble.

4

Each time Fuller returned home it seemed that Sheila had expanded a little more to fill the space left vacant by his absence. There was nothing premeditated in it. First she had learned to drive. It was necessary: after they left Oxford for the bungalow near Newbury she had to drive the children to school. Fuller wasn't there. She had joined the Samaritans and to his surprise – he never thought of her as a leader – quickly rose to a position of responsibility, receiving night-time phone calls concerned with life and death. She went to demonstrations and was something important in an anti-nuclear group. She did not talk to Fuller about these activities. A busy, quiet woman, she cleaned the house with quick efficiency before leaving for a meeting, the children's dinner already in the oven. When Fuller asked questions she was vague, suggesting it was nothing, certainly small stuff compared to his own work. It was as if she had always carried inside her a complete life in embryo which could not develop until he went away. He liked this woman but was bemused.

During the first years he had travelled less. The children ran to him on his returns and cuddled on the sofa. He lingered, knowing he would miss their touch in Kuala Lumpur or Bogotá. He caught up on their school-work and plotted with Sheila strategies against childhood problems. But in their teens the children were no longer interested in him, developing their own secrets which they thought he could not imagine and which he did not want to reveal to them as commonplace. Sheila showed a confident unconcern for their welfare – which again surprised Fuller, who imagined mothers were always anxious. He tried to find reasons for concern but could not. The children were healthy, had many friends, did well at school. They joked with him and asked for money. Sheila they treated as a friend only slightly older than themselves. His absence did not appear to harm them or to be the cause of ill will towards him.

His stays in Newbury became shorter. The garden had got beyond his control. At the pub he had nothing to say to his neighbours, all professional men with opinions. He tried to interest himself in the plays and films in London but Sheila was usually busy and he went on his own, feeling like a bachelor. There were books, but hotel rooms in foreign cities are good places to read books and there seemed no reason to reject a cabled invitation to some new assignment in some new place. Sheila accepted the news matter-of-factly, pleased for him to stay, pleased for him to go. He felt she wished him well but did not see herself as part of his good or bad fortune. For his part, he sensed he needed less and less. The money went to Sheila – his expense allowance was generous.

On one occasion he had come home to find the furnishings in the living room changed. The old lined velvet curtains were gone from the windows and replaced by bright red and orange fabric. The dining-table with dark barley-sugar legs was nowhere in the house and a table of luminous pine stood in its place. The new carpet was pale and plain, making it difficult to imagine the mellow English pattern it had replaced. Sheila had taken to wearing blue jeans and, at forty, looked good in them. He liked the new character of the house, more open and ready for action, but he sat even more lightly in it.

Once, when he told Sheila that he would only be in England for two days between trips, she had replied, 'There will always be a bed for you here,' leaving the room as she spoke and leaving Fuller to stop, consider and eventually laugh at the outrageousness of it. She cleared away his traces as she cleaned the house, deftly, automatically, her mind on other things.

Somehow the borders which enclose an adult life seemed to have exempted him, leaving him with no purpose except a purpose he might choose. It puzzled him and it was his habit on the planes back to Washington, Geneva or Rome to sift what he had seen. It was as if he had been assigned by some higher power to collect evidence on an unnamed case. What he lacked in focus he hoped to gain in reach; he could no longer refuse an invitation to any new place. Like a doctor with his patients, Fuller, the international expert, was offered the intimacies of countries strange to him. He knew little of their cultures and nothing of their histories but he knew who was corrupt and who was not, whether the money would flow or stop. The files were open to him.

In China, when he was mildly ill, the doctor, without raising his head to say hello, had simply asked, 'How's your shit?' and similarly Fuller had come to believe he would apprehend the world by leafing through its secret deals.

5

After a long time he went to fetch Regina from the bathroom. She was wrapped in two towels, doing nothing. The bath had a dark ring and there was water on the floor. She walked to the bed and sat. Fuller followed her, sat next to her and tugged at one of the towels.

'I have my period.'

Fuller took away his hand, sighed, went to speak, stopped himself. He lay back on the bed and asked what on earth she was doing picking up men in bars.

'I did not mean to go with a man. Look . . .' She reached for her purse. 'Look, I have my own money.'

'So what happened?'

'I jes' like the way you treat me.'

She talked through the night in her slow careful English. Often she went back to correct a minor point, seeming to believe her whole life would slip away if flawed by a single lie, and offering Fuller a sacred task of remembering. From where he lay he could see her silhouetted against the window. She was not quite the young beauty she had seemed – the breasts had fed babies and the flesh of her belly where he rested his hand had the texture of crushed tissue-paper. Before she spoke her tongue travelled around her lips.

'My grandmother, she was a market woman. She had money. She travelled everywhere – to Accra, to Freetown, to Monrovia . . . everywhere. My brothers and my sisters, we were five . . .'

She took her hand from Fuller's thigh to check the calculation then returned it.

'Yes, five. These are my mummy's children. My daddy, he lived with another wife and I do not know him. So we children are scattered. Myself and my sister stayed with the grandmother.

My mummy, she goes to the north. She has nothing. She is sick.

'So my grandmother cared for us. She was a good woman, very clever with business. She had a house in Kingston.' Regina checked herself. 'No, there was not always this house. When we were picins we stayed in a room near the market. Later she bought the house. I – I'—sometimes she stumbled on the 'I'—'I – I always had rice and school uniforms.

'My grandmother goes very many times to Accra. Too many times. She meets this Ghana woman and they become sisters. They were in trade together. My grandmother, she is very generous to this woman. She brings the woman's sons here to look after them, she feeds them, she buys them clothes, she pays their school fees. We are only two, my sister and myself, so the Ghana woman, she too comes to live with us.

'My grandmother becomes old and she is not strong and we have no men. The Ghana woman sends for her relations and they come and stay. They begin to push us out. Her sons, they beat me and my sisters. I am only skinny, I am only ten. They put a bad curse on my grandmother somehow. I don't know how. They pay a man to put a curse on her and she becomes ill in the head. They treat her like a beast in her own house. Sometimes they knock her down. There is no one to help us.'

For a moment Regina was silent, stroking Fuller absentmindedly.

'I have to leave this house. I must do that. From ten to fourteen – no . . . from eleven – I have no home. I sleep on the pavement or under market stalls. I have to beg for food. I don't go to school anymore. I have one dress – when I wash it I just take it off and wait in my pants until it is dry.

'When I am fourteen I meet this boy Mustapha and he is loving me. I too am loving him. I have a picin and he says he wants to marry me and I say alright. So he calls his uncle to the house.'

Fuller decided not to ask how she was back at the house.

'The uncle comes. His name is Ali. He stays and he is loving the cousin-daughter of the Ghana woman. Her name is Veronica. They tell the uncle bad things about me and he turns the boy against me so he will no longer marry me. They do not want me in my house. My grandmother, she tries to help me but they beat her. She is old and one day they beat her and she dies.'

'You mean they killed her?'

'Yes they kill her.'

In the pause Fuller heard the sound of his own breathing.

'So I have nobody. I meet one girl, Fatmata, a Fula. She is loving a Swiss man at the Sun Hotel. His name is Philippe. She says he will help me meet white men. I say, alright, I don't like Africans anymore.

'So I support my family, they all depend on me. The girl Veronica, she is married to the uncle, she is my age but they forbid her to talk to me. They say I am a prostitoot. I say, alright, I admit it, I am a prostitoot. Don't talk to me. But God will see who we are inside. Then Ali, the uncle, he died and I said to myself, you see, she would not talk to me and now her husband is dead. Now she wants to know me again. She wants to come to the Sun with me. So I just forget the past. I say, never mind what she said about me, now she has problems. If she wants to be my sister, let her be my sister. I am a good girl. I like to help people.'

Fuller wondered about goodness and where in her life Regina could have gained a store of it.

'One day this Syrian boy, he falls in love with me. His name is David. His father is rich and I stay at David's house above their shop. He says he is loving only me. He says I am very sexy. Never mind the breasts, Regina, he says, you have a nice body, you are very sexy. He says to me, Regina, I don't want anyone else to look after my pump, I don't want anyone else to eat my banana.' Now she was laughing, and squeezed Fuller's thigh roughly.

'So I live with him and have a baby for him. We are not married but it does not matter. David, he has a friend who stays with us. One day when David is not there the friend says he wants to love me. I say, no, how can you ask me that, I am loving David. But he insist. He says, Regina, I know you are sweet, I want to love you. He says that David will not mind.

'I am on the bed when David enters the room. He tells the boy to leave me alone. The boy laughs and pretends it is nothing. David, he has a small gun, but the boy just laughs. Then David shoots the gun at him, here, in the chest. The boy is so surprised he just falls down. David shoots him two more times. I tell him to stop but the boy is already dying. He tries to say something but he is already dying.

'David's family, they send me away from their house. David himself, he is sent to Valley Prison. But his family is rich and they pull him out and he is sent to Syria. I never see him again. All that time people point to me in the street and say it is because of that girl the Syrian was killed.'

She stopped, lost in an intensity of either pride or shame. She no longer seemed aware of Fuller.

'I go back to my house but they will not let me stay. They make myself and my sister live in a shack outside the house. This is my own house! This is my problem, the problem I cannot forget. Every day I see this house. It is in my head all the time. I cannot forget it. I – I hate Africans. I just want to run away from my problems. I am a good girl. I don't want to screw for money. Men fool me all the time.'

Later, perhaps near dawn, Regina stopped to wonder at her words and instead of thought found sleep. Fuller lay heavy on his back with Regina, still wearing her pants like a toddler in the street, stretched light across him, one hand burrowed in the grey hair of his chest, her cheek a damp cushion next to it. He continued to hear her voice inside his head with an absorption so complete that it was a long time before he registered the novelty of his involvement. Then he sighed and felt a sort of sadness, which he supposed was a sort of love, then, almost immediately, he felt a nostalgia for the passing of the same love. A habit of moving on. And while considering this and the wakeful night ahead of him, Fuller was, in turn, tripped neatly into sleep.

6

Fuller did not work. He sat in the lounge of the Ambassador Hotel and discovered that he knew too much. Twice there were tears on his cheeks, but he could not remember which thoughts had given rise to them – his mind had much to do and already had moved on.

In the evenings Regina came, arriving late after a long day of waiting, to find Fuller immobile and tired, alone in an armchair of ruined PVC, one of a group of chairs around a coffee table, one of a dozen empty tables in the wide tiled lounge. A pot of coffee, undrunk from the morning, was in front of Fuller, a glass of whisky from the afternoon. Regina sat; he turned to look at her and after long minutes, while the swarm of memories detached themselves from Fuller's eyes, they silently stood together and went to eat at the Paradise Gardens Restaurant and Bar, or went to Fuller's room, where he and Regina found deep sleep, their spines touching for all their length.

On the sheets of notepaper in Fuller's room was written: The Ambassador – the businessman's hotel. They lay yellowed in a drawer among the insect droppings. Few businessmen came to Kangaba now: there was no money. Those that did come stayed at the French-owned Sun at the beach, where, by presidential dispensation, everything imported could be had, a privilege denied to the government's own Ambassador. When Kangaba had prospered, the barman told Fuller on his first night, the restaurant was always full, was famous. Now it often had no food. At the reception-desk the girls slept on their arms or bullied the idle room boys, who had no rooms to clean.

The days passed over Fuller. On each side of the lounge were louvred windows from the ceiling to the floor, through which the winds to and from the sea entered and departed. The morning breeze was fresh, cooling Fuller as he sat, but in the middle hours it failed, leaving him hot and perspiring, heating and in turn heated by his embracing armchair. But he did not move. Later the wind began again, drying his sweat, sometimes strong, causing the long curtains on one side to blow horizontal and the curtains on the other to be sucked hungrily against the windows. Sometimes this wind brought rain and if no one closed the windows – as was frequently the case – a spray, a mist, enclosed Fuller, chilling him. Yet he did not move while the weather passed around him like the seasons of the year. Only the forelock of his hair broke free, resting over his eyes the way Sheila had known twenty years before – except that now it was grey – to be twisted and tugged by the careless wind.

He knew too much. In Dacca there was a Chinese restaurant – was it the Golden Duck? To get to it you went down this road and then that. He knew the way. The rickshaw man would wait for you if you gave him one or two taka. The girl who served breakfast at the coffee bar of the Dacca Intercontinental was called Matwata. Remember the names. At least the names. On the North Circular Road in London take the outside lane at the Finchley lights, you'll make up time – but move over before the next set or you'll be stuck. In Manhattan, break the red lights or risk collision from behind, but don't try it in Vienna. In Rangoon it's worth waiting for the woman at the Thai Airways office: she knows her job and is more patient than the men. ES21, G37, PV102: forms for claiming expenses from the Asian Development Bank, travel authorisations from the International Labor Office, customs declarations for America. Fuller knew all this, the dust of an official traveller and, now, as he sat stationary in the Ambassador Hotel, it blew through his mind like a desert storm which must be endured, he helpless before it, uncertain what its erosion would reveal. Swissair is best to Tanzania – try to travel on a Thursday. In Cairo never leave an office before taking tea.

It's the same in Pakistan. The Ghanaians appreciate a tie but it cuts no ice in Dar-es-Salaam. If you are with the World Bank you can get into Brazil without a visa. Avoid the Hilton in Mexico City; the Americans are noisy. In Lagos never take a taxi without first agreeing on the fare – even if it's got a meter. The business-class on Philippine Airlines is as good as first on British. A hundred bututs to a dalasi, a hundred cents to a ringgit.

In time, with the passing days, with Regina's touch, with dead nights of unknowable depth, the assault of tiny things remembered slowed, to be replaced by a gentler assault of pictures offered for his consideration – and Fuller now too worn to look away.

A taxi horse, its teeth bared in agony, the wheel of a minibus still pressing on its foreleg. It was in Senegal. Fuller had seen everything: the minibus driver, too exuberant in the traffic, had spurted forward, not noticing the horse-taxi behind the truck. The quick drama was followed by a short stillness while all those involved had wished the act undone. He had seen it from the back seat of a car and the government official next to him, noting his interest, had turned to Fuller to mention dinner. Now Fuller wondered whether the horse had been everything to the taxi-man, his only hope of livelihood, and whether the crowd had turned on the young minibus driver to stone him – perhaps to death.

In Mymensingh, in Bangladesh, the Hindus in their thousands waded into the river, floating offerings of food and flowers in front of them. The river-banks were re-created by a covering of bright cloths spread out to dry; a huge transformation requiring an immense conspiracy. At the time it was nothing to Fuller. Sitting on the raft car ferry, tired, his briefcase tight between his calves, Fuller discovered his eyes held by a man up to his neck in water, nudging before him a fragile tray of sweets and flowers. The man was of Fuller's age, his head of shiny grey hair still bearing the marks of a comb. What was the ambiguous intensity behind the man's eyes? A certainty that he was right, a certainty that it didn't matter? A pleading, yet an insistence of equal worth? A wish to impress a dignified anger before his humiliation?

It was as the man knew it would be. Fuller floated past, silent, immobile, his shoes above the other's head. The boat went on, the tray was tipped, the man was choked by dirty water among the garbage of his holy ritual. Someone laughed. Only now did Fuller wonder how there could be so many Hindus in Moslem Bangladesh.

After the second day an old man brought Fuller coffee in the mornings: instant coffee in a coffee pot, reconstituted milk lumpy in a jug and quickly sour, grey sugar-cubes. Perhaps he thought that it was for this that Fuller waited, perhaps it was a deep old habit of serving Englishmen. He said he was a cook but, 'No food, master. No food.'

In the afternoons the barman from the first night brought Fuller whisky. He drove a taxi in the day and left his passengers sweltering in the sun while he strode in to serve his only customer, the last reminder of his official job. He prised the keys from the reluctant girls at reception, went to the safe, took out the bottle of whisky, smoothly measured Fuller half a glass. Probably, when Fuller left, ambling away next to swaying Regina, the barman claimed what remained for himself – or maybe poured it back to sell again.

The cigarettes which Fuller smoked were left to burn on the table's edge and, at first, the girls at reception made their laborious way across the lounge to scold him, but soon they accepted this as a new way of things and returned to sleeping on their arms.

Somewhere in Africa there was a great tree filled with a hundred pelicans. Where? Next to a river anyway. The birds soared handsomely but landed clumsily, their webbed feet slithering on the branches. It seemed odd and wrong for water birds to live in a tree and at the time Fuller had been momentarily excited by the question, but pushed it away. He was at an official reception on a riverside patio and it would have been bad to show ignorance or doubt, even on the matter of pelicans. Where was this?

On the edge of a field of bright green irrigated rice – a car in the background with all its doors open – a single, thin farmer, cloth wrapped around his waist, feet deformed with mud, was surrounded by a knot of men, brown and white, all in crisp-ironed short-sleeved shirts. Fuller, standing back along the bund, knew the questions, knew the man was a government plant to satisfy the foreign bankers. They were asking the peasant about his income, about the number in his family, the benefits of the new irrigation scheme. He turned from one to another, rattled, increasingly uncertain what lies were expected of him, frightened of the punishments he might receive after the foreigners had left. Now, too late, Fuller wanted to intervene and comfort him, rebuke the men for their cruel game. The Philippines? Thailand? No, Indonesia. It was Indonesia.

Regina came. They ate chickenburgers and rice at the Paradise Gardens. In the morning Fuller gave her taxi-fare and she left. She did not take a taxi; he knew she wouldn't.

Finally he saw Sheila. He was inside the window of their Newbury home, she outside. Already she had pushed the children – they may have been four and six – into the little Renault Five and now was busy with her safety belt, talking all the time. Fuller's bags were by the door, his taxi due. Sheila drove away, a bit jerky, a bit fast, her short hair bouncing loose, and Fuller stole for his private collection an unauthorised memory of his wife.

Dear Sheila, he wrote in his head, if only you knew, as I now know, how much I care for you, how much I wish I had spent more time with you. Something has happened to me here – I don't know what to call it. I seem to have come to a halt . . . He could not continue, would not write it. His mind moved on.

7

In Oxford, in the days when they had known Jacob Cesay, Fuller and Sheila had been in love. On this everyone agreed.

He has not changed, thought Fuller, he is still the same old Jacob. And yet he was changed. There was the polished desk between them, behind which Jacob was rising, the name plate with the minister's name on it. The smile was still mischievous behind the bushy beard, though the beard was partly grey; the eyes twinkled, though Fuller thought they twinkled more dully, and that maybe the smile had been used too often, perhaps for the wrong purposes.

Jacob half stood and in his overeagerness was trapped between the desk and the leather chair, obliging him to fall back and try again, seeming to be the helpless victim of his wish to greet his friend. Fuller remembered the subtlety of Jacob's acting, the comprehensiveness of his charm.

In Oxford Jacob had been well-known and liked, he had always held the floor. For Fuller and Sheila he had been the witness to their love, the friend who came to dinner. If the quiet couple did not have the words to talk of their love, it was Jacob, compassionate towards his English friends, who talked for them. In company he said: 'Oh Sheila, you don't know who you are married to. He is brilliant, your husband. Sometimes he just makes me want to give up this economics business,' and for a moment he would look sad. It was only Jacob's charm but it made Sheila blush and Fuller laugh. They passed the wine. Of Sheila, he would say: 'It's not fair on the rest of us men, Hugh. How did you find her first? How can she be so clever, yet cook like this, yet be so beautiful? No, it is not possible.'

Now he swerved his way around the desk to where Fuller smiled and stood, Jacob's glamorous secretary still at his shoulder. 'My dear friend . . . can it be? How can it be? It has been so long. A lifetime.' He chuckled at the fun of it all, took Fuller's large hand in his finer one, then held it in both, then reached up to clasp Fuller's shoulders. 'Twenty years, nearly twenty years. I don't believe you have arrived.' Then, relinquishing his embrace except for Fuller's right hand held lightly in his left – Fuller feeling girlish – Jacob looked around the office for an audience and found his secretary. 'Mariatu, I want you to meet Hugh Fuller, Professor Fuller.' He chuckled again, perhaps at his exaggeration. 'My friend, teacher, colleague, brother . . . everything actually. This is a great day!' Then, not waiting for Mariatu to respond, he turned back to Fuller. 'Hugh, I don't believe you have finally arrived in my small country. It has taken you so long. What took you so long? We've needed you all this time.' Then, with a raised hand to stay the retreating Mariatu: 'Now, Mariatu, bring us something to drink. I have so much to talk about with my friend. This is about Oxford – the Isis, St Giles, so many things, that meadow . . . what was it Hugh? Never mind, we must talk. So, Mariatu, bring us something . . . drinks.' She went to speak, Fuller imagined to ask what sort of drinks, but Jacob had moved on. 'Debates, philosophy, we were brilliant in those days, weren't we Hugh? This wasn't Kingston nonsense talk Mariatu, this was Oxford, England. Please Hugh, come and sit in one of the easy chairs.' Jacob moved ahead, still nimble, though now more plump, neatly bound within the waistcoat of a three-piece suit. 'Please sit down, this is your home. Ah, Mariatu . . . whisky. Mr Fuller will have a scotch. Am I right? You see after twenty years I am still right. And a whisky for myself too. Not small ones, not official guest size. This is friendship. No . . . wait. Bring the bottle.'

When Fuller arrived in Oxford from a provincial university to take up a junior teaching job, won on merit, Jacob had been there six years and was a long-serving research student. Despairing dons who could not bring themselves to guillotine his stay passed Jacob on to Fuller as a last resort, and in the end able, conscientious Fuller had written more of Jacob's thesis than a supervisor should. In return Jacob introduced Fuller and Sheila into the social world he orchestrated around himself. Jacob's days were made up of visits. He had an Oxford bicycle – black with a wicker basket – and cycled from house to house at walking pace, a cigarette jammed between his knuckles on the handlebars, always ready to stop and chat. It was, it seemed, a delight, a joke. No one refused Jacob's presence, least of all the English girls who allowed him everything and expected nothing, making him exempt – as he was exempted from so many rules – from the restraints on other men. 'It is not fair,' Jacob had complained in mock exasperation. 'How can these girls wear summer dresses and then ride bicycles. Don't they know what they do to us?' Fuller had laughed; everyone laughed with Jacob. At debates he took the most unpopular positions and defended them with the most outrageous arguments, keeping the audience hanging with his deliberate hesitations, the unfinished sentences. His defence of apartheid at a formal debate caused a public storm, which delighted him. Self-regarding Oxford was as fascinated by Jacob as Jacob was by Oxford. At the boat races he arrived in white flannels and a striped blazer, bushy black beard concealing the tie, and Oxford was not sure whether it was mocked or honoured, but was anyway pleased to find its image in relief. For Fuller, the outsider, Jacob was a natural and a welcome friend.

'Now tell me Hugh, how is your wife, your beautiful wife?'
'Sheila?'
'Ah, yes . . . Sheila. Don't tell me you are not with Sheila. I don't want to know that.'
Fuller said that he was still married to Sheila, of course, and that she was well, but they saw little of each other these days, and Jacob said, yes, it was a shame, but it was the price of success, this curse of travel, he knew, he suffered himself. Then he laughed at the curse of his success and needed to pull down the points of his waistcoat over his small paunch.
'Ah, tha's good. Over here Mariatu . . . No, serve Mr Fuller first. Tha's good.'
There was no more talk of Sheila. Mariatu bent over them,

legs straight, left hand restraining her neckline as she poured, drawing attention to it as she knew it would, silky dress hugging her buttocks as she knew it did. Strong perfume. Jacob rested a hand on her bottom and raised his eyebrows at Fuller while Mariatu moued a token disapproval.

'She's beautiful, isn't she? You see this is what you get here when you are a government minister. A beautiful secretary.' He laughed, then corrected himself. 'Well not just here actually. All over the world. Only here we are more honest about it.' He took as much of Mariatu's buttock as could be contained in his slim hand and squeezed it comprehensively. 'But I don't think I introduced you properly. I am remiss. Now, please, I want you to both shake hands. Tha's right. Good! Hugh, this is Mariatu. She is my secretary, my right-hand man.' Fuller and Mariatu held hands at full stretch while Jacob caught his breath from laughter. 'Actually Hugh, I am not fair. She is my personal assistant, that's what she likes to be called. And Mariatu this is Hugh Fuller, my oldest friend. I want you to look after him. He's still a young man. He's still a young man isn't it?' She acknowledged with an awkward nod this clumsy code and Fuller released her hand in case she would wait for Jacob's word. 'You see, Hugh, you have made her shy. You have had an effect on her. Alright Mariatu, you can leave us now.'

The office was cool with its air conditioning, yet perspiration had seeped into the laughter-lines on Jacob's face and he seemed short of breath, leaning back now to take in Fuller's presence, while Fuller leaned forward in parallel, on the edge of his seat, toying with his glass, until Jacob, perhaps sensing a discomfort, trimmed twenty years and said, 'Don't worry about this nonsense with Mariatu, Hugh. It's part of the joke. They expect it.' He coughed and, reminded, pushed a box of long mentholated cigarettes towards Fuller before taking one himself.

Jacob's farewell party had been suitably large, all the African students had been there. In the end it had not been the university which had terminated his stay but the government of Kangaba.

Jacob's grant had always been generous thanks to an uncle's high position in the Ministry of Education, but the uncle had fallen from favour and the grant had stopped. Jacob wanted a job with the United Nations or the World Bank but an envoy from Kangaba had let it be known that a debt was owed and that without Jacob's presence at home the safety of his family could not be guaranteed.

At the party Jacob's farewell speech lasted an hour, each friend was mentioned in turn. He thanked Fuller for his help, for his hospitality and, most of all, for not being 'English'. There was a word for every person in the room and, in the end, the weight of ritual overcame his wit until it seemed that rather than returning home he was going to his death. On this occasion his famous circuitous sentences and artful stumblings seemed actually to lose their way and the twinkling eyes looked downwards, while the guests held their breath. In their gracious replies more than one African friend proclaimed that in Jacob's presence and intelligence there was the making of a great African politician, but Jacob, serious, had said, no, politics at home was not a game of subtlety and persuasion, and those who knew, agreed. Jacob, they said privately, was clever but not tough, he was too generous, he liked life too much. Fuller wondered what had happened in twenty years while Jacob's eyes had become bloodshot and his teeth discoloured.

'Oh yes, certainly I have done well enough in our small country. Not like you Hugh. You are running the world. I have only a small country to work with. They keep pushing me up. They say I am a rising man.' He stubbed out the cigarette, a quarter used, the wide gold band gleaming in the ashes. 'That's what they say. I don't know where I am supposed to rise to now. I have to be careful or Uncle will think I want to rise to his job. Then I'll be for Valley Prison. That's what Uncle does – we call our President "Uncle" – he sends his possible successors to prison. Cools them off. It's terrible Hugh really. What sort of country is this?' He shook his head and gestured his hand around the office. 'I didn't want all this. You know me. I would rather have a little cell at the university and do serious work. But Uncle says he needs me. He tells me I am the only one who can speak the language of the white tribe – that's what he calls the international financial people who come and interfere with us: the white tribe. People like you, Hugh. And how is it – your saying? In the land of the blind the one-eyed man is king. My Oxford economics is my one eye and if not king, at least minister.' Again Jacob was overcome by mirth, his body shaking, face sweating, the waist-coat riding up. 'More whisky, Hugh?' He filled both glasses, spilt some on the table top. 'Tha's right. Drink up Hugh. This is a special day. I drink too much actually, smoke too much and – you know – the girls, they just don't leave you alone. It's just not healthy. I'm in Kingston alone, you see. My wife stays with her family in the north. It's better.' He did not say why.

'But seriously, Hugh, I have troublesome responsibilities. When I heard it was you coming, my heart lifted. I know you are influential, all the aid donors at the meeting will listen to what you say. I know that. You are weighty, Hugh. You are a heavy man. Sometimes the people they send are very rude, so arrogant you would not believe it. The IMF are the worst. They send some American boy and he tells us we have to devalue the Kanga, put up the price of our rice. They talk as if we are nothing, as if they own Kangaba – it doesn't matter if our people starve. No, it's not good. I mean, I am a government minister and these people are nobodies – and they talk to me as if I am nothing just because my country is poor. And we have to take it because we need the money. It hurts, Hugh. What is a country if it cannot run its own affairs? Actually I did not learn anything of this at Oxford. Why didn't you tell me?'

'You forget, Jacob,' said Fuller, 'in those days, I had not travelled. I had only my books. I was blind too.'

Jacob looked at Fuller, wondering briefly at this punctuation, but, before it was too late, caught the tail of his own words. 'Look Hugh, look at my job. Over here, the oil price rises. Over there, your recession has lowered the prices you pay us for our iron ore. Over there, you put up the interest on the loans you pressed on us ten years ago. Where can we go? And I have to keep the farmers happy who want higher prices for their crops, the people in Kingston who want low rice prices, and then there's . . . er

. . . certain important people who become very unhappy if they don't get very rich. These are the economic affairs of Kangaba! Who would be the minister? I ask you, Hugh, would you want it?' Once more Jacob's passion turned to laughter, into which he emptied his glass of whisky, seeming, in spite of his words, to offer himself to the anarchy of it all.

'But at least I know you will understand. You are not like the clever Americans who are so ignorant. You have a heart, Hugh. And you are my friend. You see we need these extra loans these days. Uncle expects me to persuade you. How long are you here?'

Fuller replied that it was not fixed. He was not sure how long he'd stay.

'Tha's good. Tha's good. We want you to stay. Kangaba needs help from someone like you . . . Ah, excuse me. You hear that noise? It's my walkie-talkie. Uncle has given all us ministers two-way radios so we can never escape him. I'm not a free man. You can even be doing your business with a girl and Uncle will want to speak to you. It's because the telephones don't work. Mariatu . . . come here . . . Please persuade Mr Fuller to stay with us. No . . . give me the radio first. Hello . . . Dr Cesay speaking. Over . . . Yessir . . . Yessir . . . Roger. Over and out . . . You see, Hugh, it's like the army. The President wants me at the palace – some political nonsense – maybe something to do with you – I don't know. I just have to drop everything and run. Mariatu will look after you. Mariatu, give Mr Fuller a drink . . . and give him a car and driver – my other Benz. Good! And Kamara. Tell Kamara he has to help Mr Fuller with his work. He should do everything Mr Fuller asks. You're my witness . . . Hugh, it's too bad. I have to go. We'll talk more . . . you'll come to my house. It will be wonderful – like Oxford. I've given you Kamara – he's very bright. A little – how do you say? – idiosyncratic. He has his own ideas. But you remember, I was like that too. Actually he should be more senior, but, you know . . . Mariatu, my briefcase. Ah! Is that the time . . .?' He shook a thin gold wristwatch, too expensive to be wrong. 'Too many emergency meetings. It's all emergencies now. Hugh, my dear friend . . . until soon then.'

33

Mariatu, after her minister's departure, in the residual still, was immediately more collected, less voluptuous. She took away the whisky bottle, gathered up the glasses. As she wiped the table she enquired of Fuller whether there were documents which he needed now and Fuller replied that there were not. He saw that it had been for Jacob that Mariatu had swayed and stood too close, a reflection of his tastes. She called two messengers, sent one for Kamara and the other for the driver, then led Fuller to the outer office, where she sat behind her typewriter, which glowed electric.

'We were at Oxford University at the same time,' offered Fuller.

'He was your student?' Her smile was even.

'Yes – but we were friends too. He was a very senior student.'

'Yes, I can tell you are of an age.'

Fuller looked at her. She had a quality of speech which she shared with Jacob, perhaps it was Kangaban. There was a playfulness which made toys of words and made talk a shadow play which had him stumbling.

'Please, this is Latif Kamara. He'll look after you.'

Kamara was in his twenties, lithe in blue jeans, even-featured under the sunglasses which he did not remove. Neither did he step forward to shake hands, but instead inclined his ear to Mariatu while she relayed instructions and Fuller saw what he had seen many times before, the prickly pride of young men from poor countries.

'OK, no problem.' The voice was both gruff and brisk. He turned to Fuller. 'Is it Fula or Fuller?'

'Fuller.'

'I thought so. The Fula are a tribe here. The girl said Fula. She got it wrong. It's understandable. I think you can follow me.'

He left Fuller to catch the heavy door which cut off the minister's air-conditioning from the other offices.

8

Fuller's first trip outside Europe left him angry. A Pakistani student who admired his teacher had demonstrated his influence back home by inviting Fuller to advise his government. Caught up with the work of the international agencies he encountered there, Fuller found it easy to extend his trip, touching Thailand, Malaysia, the Philippines and Indonesia before returning home to Oxford. He had left Sheila for a month but did not return for three. By the time he did return – a more vigorous and suntanned man than Sheila had known – an anger had been unlocked, which, in spite of his continued outer gentleness and calm, was never again contained.

It was not the poverty that angered him, though that too shocked its way into his consciousness, it was the realization that so much had been kept from him. It was not the knowledge of the new people and places that excited him to restlessness but the extent of his ignorance. He was sure that the men at Oxford must have known that in the other places of the world the histories were larger, longer and more glorious, the people more subtly civilised, more gracious, the hospitality more open-hearted, the scenery grander, brighter, on a different scale of beauty. But they had not told him, the working-class boy from Nottingham. In every way, by every act, they had let him think that it was themselves – clever Englishmen with ash-soiled jackets and dandruff, men with money yet who counted pennies, who kept their hands in their pockets while they moved their lips, who knew and knew and knew – who were the final product of all that was best, superior men who had been justly awarded the right to judge. To the son of a mother who had no husband but who possessed an absolute belief in the redeeming power of education, these men, their grey flannels and grubby tweeds, had seemed some sort of high ground, their fluting accents some sort of call. Fuller had worked to reach them, imagining, wrongly, that he would always have to work harder than others to reach their standard, and imagining, wrongly, that by reaching their standards he would win acceptance. Instead the high ground proved elusive, the terrain shifting, no foothold firm. In the Himalayas, the light so pure that the mountains seemed illuminated from within, the sky so clean it invited him to write on it with a sweeping arm, a place which had posed and tested a dozen grand conceptions of the world while England was still mud, his anger first let itself be known to him. He said nothing on his return, behaved no differently in the common room, but when the choice was there to go away, or stay and pay his dues, he left; there was no choice.

In Indonesia the filigree ritual, when examined, revealed its Islamic present and under that its Hindu past and under that even more ancient patterns. Fuller did not stay to learn, his work carried him on, there was no one place which contained all he needed to know. He had quit his past without attachment to the future. In Africa he discovered an astonishing human grace, tightrope walkers between the body and the mind, a strange combination of language, touch and empathy. His heart swelled to know all this existed, but he did his job and moved on. The work was his accomplice, each agency only hiring him for a time, insisting that his visits should be short, just long enough to bless their works with words of economic theory. They welcomed the universal ignorance which intoxicated Fuller, none seeking complication for decisions already made. His detachment matched their gadfly ways, dipping into states but never staying, quickly drawn back into the financial atmosphere beyond terrestrial borders or calling to account.

When Fuller travelled he left not only Oxford behind but also Sheila, a blessing that genteel England had conferred on him, the best it had to offer – pretty, intelligent, the girl who could wear a pleated skirt and pearls, whose short haircuts were just right, whose breasts under cashmere sweaters were round and yielding, who knew the classics well, who told him who de Maupassant was, who maybe loved him and who he maybe loved.

There was a hint of treachery in leaving England but keeping her.

When Andrew and Melissa were three and one, and Fuller was thirty-seven, Sheila eight years younger, it was time to make a larger choice: either he continued to travel for international organisations or he stayed in Oxford to teach – the university would no longer tolerate both. And, anyway, he was always tired and had little time left for the family. He said – and believed it – that travel need only take up half the year, he would have more time with his children than a normal man. Sheila had said that she agreed: it was better that he chose to travel. And she said that if he did choose to travel she would prefer to move to Newbury – she came from there; her mother would help with the baby-sitting.

9

They crossed the wide floors of airy offices, the boards as worn as driftwood. Huddles of surly employees clung to island desks, with nothing to do, their shoes abandoned, few chairs to sit on. Kamara in his heeled boots – which must have been hot – and Fuller in his leather-soled moccasins bought in Oxford Street, made noisy progress through the bleached, bright rooms, as if only they possessed the means to cross them. Kamara scattered greetings on each side, getting willing but weary responses. 'The British gave us all this,' he observed to Fuller over his shoulder, deadpan. To a fat girl sitting with her head resting on the desk, he fired a question, got a languid reply and, reacting to that, raised a heavy shrug of laughter from her and two others nearby who shared her heat. 'She says,' reported Kamara, 'she's a typist but she hasn't got a typewriter. You might ask where the typewriters have gone. Your loans paid for them.'

On the wooden outside staircase Kamara waited for Fuller to catch up. 'You're not in a hurry Mr Fuller?'

'No great hurry Mr Kamara. Are you?'

The sunglasses crossed Fuller and passed on to the dilapidated wooden office buildings, Kingston and the forest beyond. 'I think so. I think I am in a hurry.'

'Look,' said Fuller – he had known many such young men before – 'I'm Hugh. What do you like to be called?'

'Kamara,' replied Kamara. 'I like to be called Kamara.'

'Dr Cesay has given you the best car – except for his own of course. You must be important. But of course you are old friends. Oxford, I think. I've heard of Oxford. That's where you reproduce your ruling class isn't it? Yes, I think so. You and Dr Cesay will talk the same language. Perhaps that's good.' Kamara offered

Fuller a smile of great charm and took the front seat of the car for himself.

In the Mercedes Kamara gave orders to the driver in a local language. When Fuller asked to know their destination, he replied, 'It's a visit. An errand in fact' – his language was very precise – and Fuller did not care enough to press the matter further.

The car climbed a steep, crumbling road into some poor quarter beyond street names where Fuller let purpose slip away to lie back and inspect the faces of splay-legged women preparing vegetables outside shacks of wood, tin, cardboard, anything – shacks in a living equilibrium between construction and decay. Urchins studied him back through the car window and he imagined one of them might be Regina's. The Mercedes, now well past the point where vehicles were expected, climbed potholes one by one, like handholds for a mountaineer. The driver's hand on the horn produced more gasps than warnings.

'I'm coming,' promised Kamara, leaving the car and crossing a plot of scratched maize to disappear between two houses in an alley.

'That boy is too crazy,' grumbled the driver.

'Is that right?' said Fuller.

'Too crazy,' confirmed the driver. After a pause he added, 'I'm M'bayo,' as if revealing a special quality quite different from craziness.

Fuller took in the small, ageing face with life still in it, the squinting eyes, then offered his hand and said he was Fuller, which satisfied M'bayo, who grinned and then turned back to stare ahead.

Fuller got out, unstuck the shirt from his back and tidied it over his stomach. He leaned against the car, then quickly straightened himself when he felt its heat. There were no shadows. Below, Kingston fell away to the sparkling sea and, with a small shock, he recognised the view of Kingston which had been forced on him by the airliner on the morning of his arrival. He had resisted it then; now, finding him unguarded, it made him dizzy. Perhaps it was the heat. He bent down to pick up a pebble from the dust, inspected it, dropped it. A yellow dog came near to sniff him, but not too close. Fuller thought of the hotel lounge, the passing breeze.

'OK,' said Kamara. 'No problem.' Again he took the front seat. 'Let's go.'

The car picked its way back down the road, performing balancing acts on crumbling ditch edges, tiptoeing on its disk brakes. Kamara turned around to face Fuller. 'I'll help you with your work Mr Fuller, your meetings. I'll find the reports you need. Dr Cesay always gives me the international experts. He's got no one else who will work. He depends on me actually. I know what you'll want – meetings with the Ministry of Finance, Central Bank, Trade and Industry, Natural Resources. Maybe the Inter-Ministerial Co-ordinating Committee. These are the sort of meetings international experts have. Actually, you haven't been having them. This is strange.'

Fuller pulled his attention away from the window – two little girls had stopped their play to raise hands in grave little greetings, now turned to smiles at Fuller's answering wave. 'No, I don't want any meetings yet.'

For the first time Kamara laughed – a hoarse chuckle. 'No meetings, Mr Fuller? What is an expert without meetings?'

Fuller shrugged away the question. 'I'd like to go back to the hotel now.'

'We're going. We are already on our way. You needn't be afraid of that. But Regina will not be there. It's too early for Regina.' He smiled his charming smile.

'You seem to know an awful lot, Mr Kamara.'

'I like to know everything. It's my country. Why shouldn't I know everything?'

They joined the traffic of Kingston's single traffic jam: unregulated black exhausts, crossroads with no order except that imposed by the loudest voices.

'I'll still help you Mr Fuller. I'll go to all the ministries and collect reports for you. They'll think you're working. I'll do that for you.' He laughed a second time. 'You're special Mr Fuller. I can see you are very special.'

10

The wind passed over Fuller, entering through one set of louvred windows, the curtains streaming, and departing through the windows opposite, leaving Fuller to his thoughts, only his hair disturbed. Regina came in the evenings; Kamara arrived irregularly, always at times other than those he had promised – though Fuller had not asked for promises and did not keep track. In his mind, in between long detours to places he never knew, he began letters to Sheila which he did not complete or attempt to write down. Dear Sheila . . . Dear Sheila . . . – the address whispered in the breeze which rustled the tissue papers on his table, but led only to a thousand opening sentences.

Kamara came brisk and never empty-handed. His explanations puzzled Fuller, who required no explanations and only understood that there was something to conceal.

'I've got a Five Year Plan but I think you also need the sectoral annexes. I can get the project documents for the foreign funded rural development projects but the Ministry of Agriculture needs a letter from you to release the report of the Commission of Enquiry.' Kamara had typed the letter, offered Fuller the pen. Fuller did not resist.

At each arrival Kamara carried an armful of documents from the Mercedes – M'bayo waiting at the wheel – documents familiar to Fuller: indicative annual budgets, economic projections from the World Bank, proposals for literacy from Unesco, annual reports from the boards of the ports, the railways, the para-statals for the mines. He had seen them all before; he could be anywhere. Kamara listed them but Fuller did not listen. 'Put them upstairs with the rest, Mr Kamara. Thank you.' On the desk next to his bed where he slept with Regina spine to spine, the documents covered the space and gathered two feet deep, threatening, if touched, to topple, slip and slide on to the bed, covering the bodies there. Fuller did not touch them: they could have been from anywhere.

One morning, after days and days, a girl at reception found her shoes with practised toes, pushed herself upright from her seat, lifted the lid of the counter and, without a word, shuffled across the tiles to where Fuller sat alone. She put a crumpled paper underneath the ashtray on his table and after looking at him briefly, shuffled her return, leaving only a sweet stale scent of herself and a murmured 'Mr Fuller' – the words not for attracting his attention but simply to name him, confirming the satisfactory existence of this being, who persisted and who could only be described by these words. In the mornings too, when Fuller, still dishevelled, climbed down the stairs – the lift long since broken – and arrived, the only resident, on the ground floor, they announced him liltingly to the waiting air: 'Mr Fuller,' their mouths full of his name.

Fuller ignored the paper and those that joined it – the girls at reception acting in concert to bring them to him. Some papers were white tissue, some pink, some green; all were covered in print and crumpled by many hands. It was a sort of acceptance: he was the last member of the hotel to possess them. They took their place in front of him, reminders of something passing, along with the souring milk, the abandoned cigarettes and the flicking title page of the paperback which Fuller carried down from his room each morning, placed on the table and carried up again untouched each night.

'Thief Steals Bribe', read the headline, some letters capitals, some not, some italics, some not. Fuller looked at it for minutes before he read it and it was minutes more before the words made sense. At length, he picked it up, the impulse wavering before succeeding, retreat into his thoughts as likely for a time as his arm reaching out to pull the paper free from its restraining ashtray. The columns of print were askew, Greek ruins of columns, everything irregular. 'What are Kangabans coming to? Who is behind the snatch of a case full of banknotes on its way to our President? *Flash* can only guess. If prominent Syrian grain merchants cannot pay their respects to our Head of State without being interfered with by the very security forces who are paid to protect us, what hope is there for the rest of us? Our sympathy goes to Uncle in his attempts to govern our turbulent state.' Fuller's eyes went to the heading of the page: *Flash* (Motto: the truth will out), then back to the article, which he read a second time, then to a second article – 'Our Ladies Disgrace Us' – which he also read.

Kangaba, away from the abandoned lounge of the Ambassador Hotel, was seething. There were scandals. So many that it seemed the check of public exposure had been completely and hopelessly breached, the misbehaviour flooding free without restraint. The disgraceful ladies were accountants at the Ministry of Education, bit-players in the 'Scholargate' scandal. 'Plundergate' was bigger stuff – someone had made millions signing away cut-price mining concessions to foreign firms. There was fighting in the north, a Fula marabout had led a rising. The government had kept it hush, but not *Flash* or the other tissue-paper scandal-sheets, *Arrow*, *Drum* and the ones in languages Fuller could not understand. Meanwhile in Kingston, 'Schoolgirls Tempt Top Men.' *Flash* said the men were not to blame but it printed all their names. This was reckless, heady stuff; Fuller was drawn on. A Mr Cole, once, it seemed, a Vice-President of State, had suffered 'a sudden illness', cutting his neck on a broken window while his head was temporarily confused. Another politician had been sent to cool his heels in the Valley Prison. And rice, the rising price of rice, was an issue everywhere. Rumours said the International Monetary Fund would insist on it, that Syrian traders were hoarding it, that imports were arriving, that politicians were illegally exporting it. It was politicians too, who under 'Cannibals!' were accused by *Flash* of stealing village children and eating them for their continued potency.

'Eh! Mr Fuller, that's not for you. That's for Kangabans. It's our drum for sending messages to each other. You are supposed to read the government paper, *Progress*. You are not supposed to know the truth.'

Kamara had arrived unnoticed at Fuller's table, reports under his arm. 'Every day I bring you head-loads of official documents but the first time I see you reading something, it is *Flash*. You are a mystery to me. I think maybe you are a spy, a very clever one who does not ask questions. Why am I bringing you all these reports?'

Fuller looked up. 'Because you want to read them yourself.'

'Myself?' Kamara took a step back, then laughed. 'Why should I read all this stuff?'

'Because you like to know everything going on in Kangaba – you said so yourself. And you can't get the confidential reports without my signature.'

Kamara slumped into the armchair opposite Fuller, took off his sunglasses, gave his handsome smile, slightly wry. 'Well, in fact it's true. I have to say that. You are very perceptive. In this country a foreigner like you can find out anything, but a Kangaban like me is kept in the dark. It is very interesting. It demonstrates the nature of the Kangaban state. Yes, I think so. Everything is open to people like you because you represent the real power behind the state – the foreign interests. It's people like you who keep governments in power. You should know that. Where would the government be without loans and development projects? No fat jobs for the élite, no sops to throw to the poor to stop them rebelling. That's the only reason I need your signature. I'm a Kangaban civil servant myself yet I need your signature to get these things. I don't like to have to ask you – that's the truth. It should be my right.

'What information does the ordinary population have – the proletariat, the peasantry? They are not told anything. Most of them are not even literate. Have you seen the official government newspaper? Just sport and a few lies. No free radio or television. We listen to the BBC, even though it is British – but how often does it mention Kangaba? These news-sheets, *Flash* and the rest, these are what save us. Look at them, they are shameful, they haven't even got print – and some of the writers can hardly write. Foreigners just laugh at them. But these boys risk their lives to say these things. It's true! I know these people. They all go to jail. That's how much we want our freedom.'

Kamara paused, then added in a calmer voice, 'I don't know why I am telling you this.'

Fuller looked at Kamara, who seemed exposed without his sunglasses. 'Don't worry, I'm not going to report you. I'll sign your letters, Mr Kamara.'

Kamara nodded thoughtfully to himself, then said, as if brushing away a minor irritation, 'Latif. In fact everyone calls me Latif.'

11

Three weeks after Fuller arrived in Kangaba he and Regina made love for the first time. She turned towards him as he was slipping into sleep, his night-time dreams now not so different from the day. She kissed him on his stomach, then slowly trailed her cat-rough tongue across his abdomen, along his side, over his chest and up his neck before screwing it hard and deep into his left ear. At the shock Fuller's dreams scattered.

'I am a doctor,' announced Regina intimately into Fuller's violated ear and once again applied her tongue to its task of entering his head.

Fuller had forgotten about sex; it had slipped his mind. At night Regina's touch only soothed his anxious spine. But it seemed that Regina had slept enough, her spirits were high. She was, after all, a professional.

He went to embrace her, perhaps to stay her – it was what a man should do – but she firmly pushed his arm away. 'No! Tonight I am going to work. You just lie there.' She gave a big smile.

The tongue went south, taking in his nipples, and strong fingers clasped his sex, which had lain as quiet these weeks as Fuller had sat, and kneaded it quite roughly – in spite of which it stirred.

'I am a doctor,' repeated Regina, 'I make my diagnosis,' and she sat lightly astride his chest, her back to his face, the better to attend her patient. He felt the coolness of her mouth and then its heat. He felt the point of that tongue seek out the tender spots and taunt them with its sweet abrasion.

'You see!' – Regina pulled away to look at what she had done, which was considerable, her fist now merely enclosing what before it had supported – 'You see, the cock, he always wants to fight pussy,' and here she pivoted neatly around to face him, sat back and, with only the slightest guiding touch, swallowed Fuller into herself at a single draught. 'The cock, he always want to fight pussy, but,' she confided, squeezing him, 'the pussy, she always win.'

So it was in this case. Fuller was roused into life as he had forgotten how, Fuller made corporeal, the spirit chased away – and more than once. More than once she had insisted again: 'No, tonight you lie still. I am a doctor. I make my diagnosis.'

Later, with Fuller made flesh, Fuller vanquished as predicted, now allowed to place an arm around his love, his sex returned to a dignified repose but himself not yet lost to the present, Regina, pleased with herself, elaborated on the way of things.

'You see, I am still sweet inside. I still have sugar inside. If a girl does not have sugar inside, the man will not come back. I save my sugar for my husband so I will be sweet for him. I never fuck Germans. I always say, no. They fuck too much, they go on for too long. The Germans at the Sun, they have plenty of money but I never go with them. Even if they insist. If a girl fucks with Germans she will use up all her sugar. I still have my sugar for my husband.' She reached down to check the truth of this, then snuggled up to Fuller.

PART II

12

One evening Kamara arrived at the Ambassador without a pile of documents and without the ministry car. He went straight to Fuller. 'Come on, it's time you got out of that chair. It's time you found out about Kangaba.' Fuller hesitated and Kamara, agitated by the possession of some sort of decision, stood over him. 'Come on, let's go outside and move around Kingston. If you are thinking about Regina, don't worry about her. She will wait for you. She spends her life waiting anyway.'

The road down from the hotel was the best in Kingston, with a line of jacarandas on one side and the high wall of Government House on the other. Kamara was silent, then said, 'yes,' and later 'yes' again. Fuller waited, concentrating on his stiff legs and the uneven surface of the road. There was no traffic and the few people out after dark kept the jacarandas between themselves and the sentries by the wall. Only Kamara took the centre of the road and when he finally asked, 'What do you know about Kangaba?' his tone was aggressive, like an awkward young man resenting his need to court a girl.

Fuller said he knew little about Kangaba, hardly anything at all. 'I'm a real stranger. I don't even know the meaning of the name.'

'Good!' But the words were still blocked and when at last they came Kamara offered everything at once, in a confusion of facts and reservations. Only after they had passed the law courts and were among the shops and offices did he relax and then his words, delivered loud into the night, seemed to calm him.

'All right, I'll tell you about the name. It's an accident actually. Well, not an accident, nothing is an accident. It is because of our colonial history and that was no accident. That was because of social forces in your country I think. Yes, that's what I think. We chose Kangaba in 1960 when we became independent. Why should we be called The Grain Coast? Why grain? For who?

Why coast? We reach four hundred miles from the sea. Someone came up with the name Kangaba because Kangaba was a kingdom in West African history and it somehow overlapped with the north of this country. I think it was a good choice, actually. OK, I'll tell you something about the old Kangaba because it is a good lesson – it shows how you turned our history inside out. I got all this from books. I made it my business.

'Kangaba started a thousand years ago. It was a small kingdom of traders somehow related to my own people, the Mandinka. The big state at that time was the Ghana Empire which surrounded the south of the Sahara. Nothing to do with present-day Ghana – forget that. It was a great civilisation and Kangaba sold gold to Ghana which traded it across the Sahara to Egypt and Europe. You got your gold from us. We had a great civilisation here and where was England a thousand years ago? Nowhere, I think. Our empires have always been around the Sahara, the coast was nothing. Only in your version of history where you discover us is the West African coast important.

'So, that was Kangaba. Nothing much happened until the Ghana Empire began to disintegrate. Then Fula tried to take over and Kangaba had a hard time with them. There are stories about the taxation and the way they treated our women. These are the same Fula who are troublesome in our country now. Very arrogant. They are poor yet they think they are very superior. If you don't have cattle the Fula think you are nobody and they believe they have the word of Allah. Honestly, I have to tell you about this tribalism. It is a terrible thing in Africa, the way it prevents the development of class consciousness. And Islam too, that's another thing that keeps people's eyes closed. I want to tell you about that too. OK, I'll come back to it . . . Anyway, the Kangaban people rebelled and this time they gave the Fula a real beating. This was a long time ago – history. Thirteen something in your years. It all happened far north from here, past the Futa Jallon Hills. The Kangabans found a leader called Sundiata Keita who defeated the Fula leader Sumanguru. This was the beginning of the next great West African empire, the Mali Empire, so it was important. The name Kangaba got lost in the name Mali, but Kangaba was the start of something great. That's why people thought it was a good name at independence. But a name is not enough. Of course not everyone wanted it – the Fula didn't and the foolish Creoles in Kingston wanted an English name. I want to tell you about them sometime; they are a sad case in Africa.

'Anyway, between the two Kangabas there was a lot of history. Mali came and went and we had more troubles with the Fula. In the eighteenth century they became aggressive again and set up a religious state in Futa Jallon, under the excuse of a Moslem holy war. Lots of people fled and there was a chain reaction with all the tribes fighting each other for territory. By this time the Europeans were trading on the coast and you made everything worse. OK, I am trying to put everything into the picture and it just gives me a headache. Can you imagine, things happening in England, France and Portugal determining what happened somewhere way inside Africa? Because of your slave trade you encouraged all the wars in this part of Africa – the more wars, the more captives for you to buy. You just sat on the coast and waited for us to bring slaves to you. Trade started to move towards your ships instead of across the Sahara. There was bloodshed and chaos instead of civilisation. All this because of something happening inside England. Fifteen million people sold as slaves! That's what I read. We have never recovered. When I meet white people and they say we need help to run our affairs it makes me angry. They say we are primitive, but it was you who took all those slaves. When I was a schoolboy I joined a riot – actually I was a ringleader – and we attacked some white people. In those days I was racist, I had no analysis. One old businessman had the cheek to stand up and tell us that he was there to help us. I made sure he got the biggest beating.

'During all this history the Mandinka were scattered everywhere. You'll find us all over the country – traders, koranic teachers. It's only in the far north we are a majority. We even traded slaves, like the others. I have to say that is true. There are even stories in my own family. Oh yes, I'm coming now to the Creoles.

53

When you did not want slaves anymore and changed your laws you just dumped those you had on your ships. Those are the Creoles. They come from all sorts of places in West Africa, not just from around here. Others, you sent back from America. I'll tell you what you did because it is typical. Some of those slaves fought for you during America's war of independence and you promised them land in Nova Scotia and New Brunswick – Canada, I think. We know these names because some people in Kingston still know they came from there. But of course you just kept them there – I think it is a very cold place, very, very cold – and did not give them land. Then one day, after years and years, you put the survivors on boats and sent them to Kingston. They didn't belong here, they did not belong anywhere. They are our confused Creoles, not Africans and not Europeans. Very reactionary in politics here because they can't identify with ordinary Kangabans. You see how you loaded us with problems?

'All those days there was still no country here, just tribes and small kingdoms. In the south our traditional religious organisation – "poro" – helped hold us together and in the north Islam was at least something. You did nothing but sit on the coast and encourage social disintegration. You only got interested in colonising us when the French started claiming land on each side of the Kingston coast. Then you sent soldiers and missionaries to finish us off. The Grain Coast was a deal you made with the French in 1895 – that's all. Lines on a map. That's our country. That's Kangaba. An upside down chaos of peoples who hate each other because you made them hate each other, a destroyed society just held together by your bit of bureaucratic government, just enough to let a few people get rich without changing anything. Yet we get all these development workers who think they are so great and we can't do anything. Even our own people can't do anything.'

They reached the empty harbour and Fuller, feeling weak, sat on a mooring post. Kamara sat next to him and was silent. Then, 'I had to tell you this. I don't know why. I don't want you to misunderstand my perspective just because I am friendly to you.'

'It's OK. I'm interested.'

Kamara nodded, then stood up. 'Of course you can never really understand.'

With his monologue expelled and Fuller still Fuller, Kamara lost his decisiveness. He looked back up at the town, his eyes moving from one light to another with a show of attention until Fuller took the lead by standing and wryly bending and unbending a stiff leg. 'I think you had better show me the way back up the hill, I'm not used to moving around, you know.'

13

Dear Sheila,

I've been writing to you in my head off and on for the past few days and I thought I'd try and put something on paper. It's odd, I can't remember ever writing you a serious letter before. Either we were together or it was postcards. I've no idea whether you will be listening. I suppose it will be strange for you to receive this.

I don't know where to start. All I've written in the last fifteen years are reports. All I know is that I want to explain something to you. I keep starting 'Dear Sheila . . .' in my head.

Well, the facts. Something seems to have happened to me. I arrived in Kangaba three weeks ago on a fairly routine job and I haven't done any work since. Maybe this is what people call a breakdown. Looking back on the past few weeks my behaviour must have been odd – although no one here seems to have minded. All I've done is to sit in the hotel lounge and think. Well, not even think really – thoughts have just come to me without me asking. It's as if I was in a line of traffic and I stopped too suddenly. All the cars behind have been crashing into me. All the places I've been to and haven't had the time to take in have caught up with me. I feel battered and a bit dizzy. This is the first time I've picked up a pen since my arrival. But I don't feel ill. I don't really feel disturbed. I just feel the world has taken me over instead of me controlling it. I don't know what to make of this. So maybe it isn't a breakdown after all. Maybe it's normal. I wouldn't want to overdramatise it. Anyway you mustn't worry. I'm all right and people here have been helpful. Jacob Cesay is here, incidentally – the same Jacob we knew in Oxford. I'd forgotten all about him until he made contact. He's the Minister of Economic Affairs – what they call a 'big shot' here. He asked after you. He still says how lucky I am to have you as my wife, just the way he used to.

But this isn't what I wanted to say. There is something I wanted to say but somehow I can only write around it. Something stops me getting to the centre of things. It's about us. I want to reach you again somehow. I know that our separation has been my fault. I've been caught up in my work and you have had to look after things on your own. We were never much good at explaining things to each other. Perhaps that's just part of being English. I've never known what you really wanted – you've never complained. When you did something it has always come as a surprise to me. And to be honest I'm not sure I've known what I wanted either – and you've never asked. Oh, this is difficult. I just don't know whether you are interested Sheila. You will probably put this straight into the wastepaper-basket. For all I know you may have secretly hated me all these years. Was it all me or was it you too? And what about Andrew and Melissa? I've hardly seen them since they became teenagers. It's extraordinary, yet nobody ever raised the question. It's only just struck me as strange.

This is no good. I suppose all I can say now is that I don't know where I go from here. I'm just waiting and seeing. For once I can only let the world come to me. There doesn't seem any basis for decisions anymore. I've been paid to make judgements for all my working life. Now it seems mad. Yes, really. I think my work has been mad. I've been making decisions on the narrowest of grounds – nearly everything important was excluded. It must be madness to live in such a world. You just don't realise it's mad when you are paid so much. You know, almost none of my calculations has ever come true – governments didn't get the return on investment I calculated and the effect on the population was always different from the projections, but nobody ever criticised me for it. Curious. It suited the governments and the development banks to pretend it would be true. One always wanted the money, the other always wanted to lend it. Everyone was happy. I got paid. I knew the world was different but I did it anyway. It's mad, Sheila.

Now I've started lecturing. I can't get to what I really want to talk about. Maybe the trouble is that we were never really close

— there's nothing to go back to. I don't know if I'll send this. I don't know when I'll leave Kangaba. Please don't worry. Bear with me.

Hope the anti-nuclear work is going well. Love to Melissa and to Andrew.

Love, Hugh

14

Rice Riddle

Our sleuths have been working day and night on the mystery of the missing rice. Last week we saw the ships. Our dockworkers worked hard breaking their backs to unload two big shiploads. But where has the rice gone? Interviews with market women proved that they had no rice to sell. The storekeepers at the government stores say they have not been authorised to sell rice. On Thursday a thousand people turned up with their sacks and bowls and paraffin cans at the harbour warehouse to be told that they had been victims of a cruel deceit. At the Ministry of Food where the army has been put in charge of food distribution they say the rice is being kept for emergencies. But we have to tell you: the emergency is here.

The only rice we could find was on the black market where a sack large enough to feed a family for a month costs one hundred Kangas. As we all know a government clerk only earns eighty Kangas a month. How can he live? And this is not to mention that government salaries have not been paid for months. How can men be honest in times like these?

In keeping with our motto, 'The truth will out,' we find it our duty to inform the President that his people are in pain. He should not listen to those who stand between himself and the ordinary people who trust him. The uncertainty gives rise to vile rumours. The most shameful of these is that Uncle has used the rice to pay his ministers and that the trucks we hear at night are taking the rice across the border. We his loyal journalists ask the President to show his people the rice and squash this smear on his reputation. Let there be no Ricegate in Kangaba.

Flash, September 1st

15

'I like Latif. I like him to be my brother. When we were young we went to the same school. This was before the Ghana woman came. My grandmother and Latif's aunt were sisters. He was cared for by his aunt. I don't know about the mother. In those days our family was strong. My grandmother was the leader of a group of market women – they all look up to her. Latif's aunt respected her even though they were sisters from the same age group. When they put a curse on my grandmother and our family went down, my sister and myself had to leave school and I hardly saw Latif any more. He was my senior; I used to follow him to school. In truth we are shamed, we do not like to see our schoolfriends. But I always walked past his aunt's house. All the time I was a girl I walked past this house. At that time they were still poor, they just shared a room with some relatives, but his aunt, she had this piece of land next door – just grass and weeds. She always had this land. She looked after this little piece of land. Each year she cut back the grass and planted a few bricks on it. Bricks cost too much. You hardly see houses made of bricks. At first you could not find the bricks at all. As soon as she planted them the weeds would cover them. But she must have gone back because the bricks grew up. I walk past this plot all the time when I was a girl. Some years the bricks were higher than the weeds, then some years she would not plant any bricks and the weeds would catch up. Nobody believed that it would ever be a house. Then the walls were as tall as me. I was eleven. I was still small. I just stood and looked at the walls for hours. I do not know what they meant to me. At this time my sister and myself, we had no home. We were going down. We were poor. Honestly, I spent hours just looking at the brick walls of this house. I could not understand how some people go up and some people go down. Then the house was finished all of a sudden. Latif's aunt became rich and one year she bought a tin roof and the ground was cemented. They built a high wall around the compound so I could hardly see in anymore. That's where Latif lives now, with his aunt. And I know he finished school. He is very intelligent. I know it. Everybody where we live respects him even though he is only young. They ask him to their houses for advice on their children and government business. They do not do that with any other young man. The others are all vagabonds. They just hang around and worry people with their thieving. Then they drink too much. Latif never wants anything from you. The others, they just want to screw you and then give you nothing. They think so just because they are young men. If I meet Latif he always treats me with respect. He says, "Hello Regina Touray." Always that: "Regina Touray", not just Regina. And he looks at you. He stands straight and looks at you like this and listens to what you say. I always want to see Latif but he makes me shy. He is very scarce these days. He is too busy. I do not think that boy is afraid of anybody. No. Let any policeman or somebody give us trouble, he always has the words.

'I talked with Latif just after I had first met you. It was the exact same morning after I first met you. I was walking home. I was just thinking in my head – I did not want to go home. I knew my sister would abuse me because I had been with a man but I had brought no money. I was just walking slowly and I heard his voice. He has a good voice. He says, "Regina Touray I must talk to you." He said that he never saw me these days. I did not know what to reply to him – I was still in my head. He always surprises me. Then he asks me about my uncle. I have an uncle who was arrested. He is a member of a trade union. Latif asks who arrested my uncle and what do they do to him. I told him my uncle is all right, he is back in his house. It was only the ordinary police that arrested him, not the SDF. He was only given a small beating. Then Latif asks me about you. He already knows that I am loving you even though it is the first time – I don't know how. I say you are a kind man. I told him that. I knew that. Then he asks some questions I do not know. How long you are staying? What is your work? I say I do not know. I say you are a quiet man. I say to him, "Do men and women talk about work in bed?" Latif is like that. He likes to know everything. I think he is somehow interested in politics. I think he wants to help poor people. Most people think that about him. Because of that my sister tells me I should not talk to him, but I like him to be my brother.'

16

Sheila had been one of the girls in the flat upstairs – the one who was not silly. When he arrived at Oxford at twenty-eight for his second job – at the first he had made a reputation publishing articles on economic theory which left even his own mind dazed – Fuller took a ground-floor flat in a big house in north Oxford, the centre of the university community. He was big, good-looking, women liked him, he felt himself successful. He knew he had worked for what he had won. In spite of all this and in spite of being surrounded on all sides by lively youth, he found himself without a lover. Oxford life passed him by and he settled for work. He guessed the girls above him – students, yet he felt more knowing than himself – talked about him and once he accepted an invitation to tea, a ritual affair in front of the gas fire, complete with cakes and the girls enticingly casual, but always more with each other than with him.

Sheila, the quietest of the three, demure in tailored skirt and short fair hair, was studying English literature. She was the one who later found time to smile and pass the time of day while she parked her bicycle in the hall. It was her final year and Fuller was impressed by the lack of panic. She was a prize he had not known he wanted, a soft-curved beauty of the middle-classes, a girl of wit and composure, the daughter of a solicitor.

They became lovers after her final exams, in the lame weeks that ended her Oxford student life. She took the lead, told him he was special, was fierce in placing him above the average Oxford man, never mind their arrogance. Then she revealed to him that underneath the trim clothes and efficient manner there was a wonderful recklessness that had them in bed and making love in the afternoon while her friends upstairs only talked of it and, several times, had them nearly caught compromised in public places. She said she loved his big body, the large features of his face, his slow unathletic strength. She said she loved his ironic humour and told him in a romantic way that she had found in him a secret sadness which made her love him.

After the summer Sheila went to Durham University to research D. H. Lawrence but – the same recklessness – chucked it in at Christmas and returned to Oxford to be with, and marry, Fuller. It was said they were a lovely couple and they secretly agreed.

17

'Regina?' Kamara looked away before continuing. 'Actually that killing had nothing to do with her. It did not concern her. She just likes to believe it did. I know these girls – they have no analysis. They are an underclass actually. Yes, it's true! Regina Touray! . . . When we were small we went to school together, then something happened to her family. She was quite unfortunate. I don't know the details. In a way you will not understand, she is still my sister because my aunt and her grandmother were members of the same branch of the bundu – the women's secret society. It means something here. Quite a lot actually. Her family went down. I think maybe they are ashamed. She's a prostitute, actually. That's the truth of it. You should know that. These people are exploited, they are victims, but they do not see it that way – they are not politicised. It hurts me – it hurts me here – to see how blind they are.

'Actually the murder is an example. Now I think of it, it is a very good example. She thinks the boys were fighting over her – that it was jealousy. This is all she knows. They just see the world like that. In fact it was all about economics – that's why people fight each other. Regina was just there by accident. She thinks she was the centre of it but she is fooling herself.

'The boy who was killed was a Lebanese from Nigeria. You know the Lebanese are the big exploiters here – we call them Syrians but it's the same thing. They are the bourgeois comprador class here. You know these terms, you're an economist. I think you must know Marx. Anyway they act as the local representatives of foreign exploiters. They run the country, actually. That's the sad truth. Uncle is nothing without them. In Nigeria they have tried to throw out the Lebanese traders – the indigenous compradors wanted a bigger share of the exploitation. Yes, I think that's the correct analysis. This boy was from a Nigerian Lebanese family which wanted to settle in Kangaba and the family of

Regina's boyfriend was their local contact – they were distant relatives. The boy came with a lot of money. A lot! I know that. But he was too clever. It was a falling out of thieves. I think that's what you say. The family here already had the Datsun import concession – it costs a lot of bribes to get import concessions here, then you make your fortune. They were helping the boy to get permission for new car imports – Subaru, I think. Something smaller. You know, they had to give money to the President and the ministers and so on. This is the way it is here. But the boy did a very foolish thing. He made his own deal with the government to restrict the imports of other cars while he got started. In fact it was my own minister who was involved, your friend Dr Cesay. Yes, I'm sorry but I have to tell you that. Anyway, when the boy's relatives found out he had tried to cheat them, they had to punish him. Regina just happened to be in the room. That's the truth. It was even in the news-sheets – *Flash*, *Messenger*, *Arrow* – but still Regina doesn't believe it. She thinks it was about her and love. You see, it's an illustration – people refuse to understand things beyond their power. That is why they have to be politicised. They have to bring everything within their power so they will not be afraid to open their eyes. They need to be organised. I believe that. I believe that so much.'

Kamara dropped his eyes to the table top where his hand gripped the edge, then relaxed.

'Later Uncle let the boy go free. He was supposed to stand trial but his family paid something. The President called it "cutting judicial red tape". It's true!' He got up from the table and started to walk away, more out of agitation than purpose. Then he turned back to Fuller and said angrily, 'We've got no sort of justice here.'

18

Once, in the Philippines, Fuller had found himself strangely alone on a country road. The Toyota Land Cruiser had broken down, the driver had gone for help. It was unusual for Fuller to be alone in a foreign place: there was always an official. The road was quiet – only the occasional truck. On each side were paddy fields, bright with the unnatural green of green revolution rice. In the distance peasants bent like commas. Bordering each side of the road were strong trees, regularly spaced by some past power with a taste for order.

A wide American car, once white, approached along the straight road, bouncing rhythmically on its worn suspension. Without reason, while still a hundred yards from Fuller, the car swerved and hit a tree head on, without fuss, as if it had found its target. Fuller remained still for a full minute before he moved, running then towards the buckled, broken car. He had not been sure he was in this scene, he had needed to reason it out. Inside the driver was alone, unconscious. The laminated windscreen was cracked where his head had struck. Fuller was sure the man was dead and wrenched the bent door free with all his strength.

The driver had only broken his wrist. Farmers from the neighbouring fields arrived after Fuller and clustered around, abusing the man for drunkenness. At first they looked to Fuller to see whether he would take charge, but when he did not their Filipino voices became loud and the growing crowd pushed Fuller to its edge, as flesh extrudes a splinter.

Later the crash reappeared, changed, in a dream. In it Sheila was with him when the car crashed. There had been more blood, the driver had been terribly injured. Sheila had run recklessly towards the car, down a road now busy and dangerous with dirty, violent, feuding trucks. It was as if she loved someone in the car. Fuller had run after her, catching her in time, pulling her away from the road towards a red phone box built in the English style. It was typical of him, thought Fuller when he recollected the dream, that he should want to call for help. They crowded into the phone box, Sheila shaking now, but trusting Fuller, deferring to him. He turned out his pockets and tried coin after coin, but they were all foreign, none fitted the slots.

19

'Ah, that business with the Lebanese.' Jacob shook his head and shifted on the couch as if trying to find a proper setting in which to place his story. 'No, the girl was not involved . . . You know, Hugh, sometimes things happen here which I do not like. Being a politician isn't like being an economist – you get involved in things.' His hands slowly shaped these things as if they were women. 'Look, I'll tell you the truth of that story. But you are not to say a word. I just want you to understand my problems.' His glass was empty of whisky; he filled it.

'The boy was innocent – the one who was killed. Ah, I don't even like to think of it. In fact in a way I killed him. Yes! But what could I do? I'll tell you. These Syrians, they bring their money straight to Uncle. In suitcases even. Can you believe it? They are very crude. Uncle takes the money and tells them it is OK for them to import the cars – he does not even think of economics. Honestly Hugh, it's terrible. Please never say a word of this – this is between friends. It's not for your reports. I have to keep all these things to myself – that's why I drink so much of this. You just don't know – nobody's life is safe here.

'I told Uncle we cannot increase our car imports. It's against the agreement with the IMF. We don't have the foreign exchange – and so on. I try to be very soft about it but I can see he is angry – he has already taken the money you see. Then he has an idea. He is very cunning. He tells me that if we can't increase imports for the new Subaru concession then we must reduce the quotas of the other car importers. And he makes me responsible! He said, "You are Minister of Economic Affairs. This is an economic affair."' Jacob shrugged. 'The Syrians were very angry. Then Uncle calls me to the palace again. He says, "Jacob, this new Syrian boy, is it true that he will benefit from the cuts in the quotas of the other importers?" I said, "Yes. Of course it is true."

So he says, "Then he should pay. I want you to collect some more money from him. Import Licence Fee."

'I had to do it, Hugh. You can't refuse the President. Then he did a terrible thing. He somehow let people know that the boy had paid me a bribe to reduce the import quota of the other Syrians. The news-sheets published it. My name was there. To this day everyone thinks I helped the boy try to cheat the other Syrians. Of course his relatives had to kill him. You see how cunning Uncle is? That's why he keeps in power so long. He had taken all the money and then made the Syrians kill their own brother. Everyone was happy – the other car importers got their old quotas back.' Jacob paused, then laughed wildly. 'Then he calls me to the palace again and tells me I shouldn't worry about my part in it: he'll protect me from the anger of the Syrians. Can you imagine!'

'So Regina was nothing to do with it. She was just left with the murderer's child by accident.'

'Regina? The girl? No, she was nothing in this.' Jacob returned to his thoughts.

'She's my friend, you know.' Fuller looked away from Jacob. 'She seems to have bad luck. She told me that her boyfriend had to leave her because he killed someone out of jealousy, but I find it was not about that at all – it's all about business and bribes. Even the IMF is somehow involved. I don't know . . . each time I learn something new about Kangaba the explanations are bigger. They seem to have no borders. There seems to be no basis for dealing with things in Kangaba.' Fuller looked up but met only a drunken vagueness in Jacob's eyes – he had not been listening.

'Tha's right. Tha's right,' soothed Jacob. 'It's terrible, Hugh. It's horrible.' Then, pulling himself together: 'That girl isn't right for you, Hugh. You should have someone better. I will find you someone.'

20

Our Women are Dying

Tragedy entered the Ricegate saga this week. When will Uncle act? Now it is our women who are dying. The Kingston market women took to the streets last week and marched on Government House singing their songs of mourning and supplication. *Flash* talked to their spokeswoman Amie Kamara before the disaster who said they had to act because they, the market women, had been the target of the people's fury. People are angry because they can only sell rice above the official price, but it is not their fault that the government will not release rice for them to sell.

The women never guessed that they would be physically abused by the President's own SDF boys and two of their number battered to death. What is happening to us when we are killing our own women? All attempts by *Flash* to discover what caused these boys to run amok met with official stonewall. We ask our President seriously, please tell us that the SDF is under control. Ricegate is tearing our people apart. How can hungry men be reasonable?

Flash, September 8th

21

Dear Sheila,

I woke up this morning angry at you. I can't remember ever being angry with you before. I suspect it now. I'm sure I'm in the wrong but the feeling is strong and it might mean something so I will tell you. I'm angry because you let me go. Why didn't you ever ask me to stay? Why didn't you find out whether something was bothering me that kept me away? You must have seen that I've been lost all these years, why didn't you help me? I couldn't help myself. Instead you just turned your back and got on with your own activities. Even the children learned to make do with just you, so there was nothing left for me when I returned. You froze me out. I was already out in the cold in my aeroplanes, hotels and the offices of international organisations and you never tried to bring me back. You just let me go. Why did you do that?

On my last visit to the Philippines I met someone who knew you. I had never met him before. He implied that you disapproved of my work, as if I was on the wrong side. But you never told me what you thought. You're involved in CND and that sort of thing so you must have political ideas but you never told me what you were thinking. Maybe I have been doing harm all these years working for development banks and aid agencies – maybe I have been nothing more than an agent of Western powers and repressive governments. I don't know. This is just the way the world works. You could have helped me, Sheila. When we were young I think you did love me but then you just seemed to lose interest. Maybe that's the real reason that I didn't come home any more. But even then you didn't say anything. It might have been better to ask for a divorce or at least complain. We've crippled each other by being married but not married. I might have fallen in love with someone who cared. You might have found someone who shared your interests.

I just needed to say all this. Take it with a pinch of salt. I know even as I write it that it's unbalanced and self-indulgent. And probably it's unfair on you. But maybe it will help you understand what is going on in me. Maybe make you think. I'm not equipped to talk about emotions. I feel that, at fifty-one, I am entering totally strange territory. I'm very naïve and I don't know any of the laws. I'm illiterate in emotions. I suppose I should say I have a girlfriend here. We haven't got much in common — she's a simple girl but I'm touched somehow. Everything is surprising me these days.

Don't be angry.

Love, Hugh

22

Uncle, they say, will never die. If he was going to die he already would be dead. Those who keep count say he is well over eighty, but no one knows the year when he was born. Some say that he is kept alive by injections, others that it is through the sacrifice of babies by the infamous leopard society. Nobody is sure. His face has turned to stone, the man has long left the shell; what remains is the home of the spirits from whom he purchased immortality.

Jacob knew Uncle's doctor, a small, bald man, always anxious. Young girls, never older than fourteen, were, it seemed, sometimes taken to the presidential palace and, after the doctor had infused the presidential body with powerful injected chemicals, they were, reputedly, impaled on an unnaturally rigid member which did not change from beginning to end and which made no answering movement in response to the efforts of the girls. Nor did Uncle speak, or comfort them in their task. The girls were returned to their families speechless and marked for ever. Some never made love to another man and, it is said, at least one released her hold on life to waste away and die.

In the photos which were in every government office, restaurant and bar, Uncle did not smile or even trouble to assume a statesman-like expression. He looked ugly and battered and absent. His clothes appeared awkward, as if he was a statue dressed by other hands and which turned out not to conform to human proportions. Recently, for reasons of political expediency, he had become a Moslem but even the loose robes of this new guise failed to make him appear an ordinary man.

His speeches were few and enigmatic. When he opened parliament he encouraged the MPs – all hand-picked – to be more corrupt, to serve first themselves and then the country. Yet later the same day a minister previously believed to be in favour was beaten by thugs and Uncle let it be known that greedy politicians

74

who abused their powers could not be protected from popular justice.

Eight years earlier the ineffectual commander of the Kangaban army, Colonel Perkins, a man who stuttered and who had been chosen for that trait, attempted a coup for no better reason than to give his job a purpose and to defy some teasing friends. It was clear that Uncle knew the coup attempt was coming. He slapped it down with a few foreign troops imported for the purpose and confiscated the army's ammunition, locking it up underneath his bedroom in the basement of the presidential palace. The officers were executed except, out of cruelty, Colonel Perkins, who was left as head of the army and was left to spend his life stuttering and drinking in the decaying building which had once been the British Officers' Club. Now there was a Special Defence Force – the SDF – with no officers except those street leaders who had the passing favour of the President and no uniforms except red berets.

Uncle, Jacob said, was a clever man, Kangaba an unruly place to govern. It would be wrong, Jacob said, to imagine that senility had robbed Uncle of his cunning. Everything in Kangaba was still his to dispose. The Syrian businessmen needed Uncle more than he needed them. Even if foreign governments and the IMF withdrew their loans Uncle would endure, the last of the old African leaders understood by old Africa. Fuller should meet Uncle. If Fuller wanted, Uncle could give Fuller a place in Kangaba for ever – a luxury house on the beach, a brief to occasionally advise on international financial affairs, to keep in contact with friends in high places. Jacob had already spoken to Uncle, a visit would be arranged. He had to go; Uncle was expecting it. He wanted to meet Fuller. It was more than Jacob's life was worth if he did not.

23

For twenty years Sheila had been the only woman, but in his late forties, when he recognised his detachment from Newbury, Fuller began to take lovers. He was more in Washington than in England, he visited offices in Manila, Rome and Geneva more often than he visited his home. The lovers were mostly of a type, career women in their middle years who valued their self-sufficiency and had long since shed the idea that sex was more a favour to the man than to themselves. They were smart, cultured women.

Monique in Washington was French, once an anthropologist in Africa, now an administrator of loans to Third World nations. Still chic, she cooked him deft dinners and suggested shows at the Kennedy Center. If she was busy, or another lover was in town, she told him so with a directness which was American and a tinkle of laughter which was French. Once, like a small girl, she had told Fuller on her pillow that he was pretty and they had both laughed at terming his strong features so. And once, in an off-hand way, she had asked him why he did not get a permanent job at headquarters.

The Filipino girl in Manila – it was difficult not to have a girl in Manila – was the exception: young, a sales clerk in a tourist shop. While Fuller dithered over a present for Sheila – nothing ever seemed right – she had taken him in hand fiercely, insisting from behind a pretty smile that he tell her the name of his hotel. She had arrived the same evening and within minutes had bullied the management to change his room from one overlooking the road to one overlooking the pool – 'He's an important man!' Soon she had befriended his secretary and won a promise to be told of Fuller's arrivals. In taxis Fuller had to fight to stop her paying and when he protested at her expensive presents she sulked. Her jealousy alarmed him: he felt sure she would fight with her nails in some smart restaurant because of a woman's glance. He could not imagine what she was fighting for.

In Rome there had first been an American and then an Italian, in Geneva an Indian. For several years he collected lovers, touched and confused by their affection for him. He departed from them in the same way he left countries: wondering, grateful, sad in the belief that they really wanted something other than he had given – and that the nature of this something was concealed from him. Then, more recently, without knowing why this clearance should be necessary, he had put each of them aside, gently, systematically, as a labourer might put aside a nest of kittens, conscious of the roughness of his hands. He hoped he hadn't hurt them, the friendship had been fine but it wasn't what he was looking for, his heart wasn't in it, he had better stay alone. The career women said it didn't matter, though they couldn't see the reason why. Only the girl in Manila had made a fuss. She said he was crazy and maybe homosexual too.

24

The basement had been a school. 'It was used by the Catholic church,' Kamara explained. Kamara was always explaining. 'I think they are not allowed to hold classes anymore. The Moslem thing. I went to a Catholic school myself – the Jesuits. Somehow they still like me. It's strange actually. They let us use the room for our literacy classes.'

The room was in an old, square house near the docks. On either side were warehouses, locked and barred after dark, with scrawny watchmen squatting on the ground outside, small fires, the weapon of their superstitious choice nearby – a stick, a farming knife. The three-storey building must have been one of the first on the waterfront, the proud office of a British colonial trading company, filled then with clerks at high desks who had been led to Kingston by reckless ambition. Fuller imagined all this. Now the plaster was falling away in chunks sufficiently large to kill a passer-by and it was hard to imagine, in Kangaba, an enterprise orderly enough to match the three rows of shuttered upstairs windows.

'What's the rest of the building used for?'

'Upstairs? It's the police.' Seeing Fuller's face, Kamara laughed. 'They don't bother us. It doesn't work like that.'

The schoolroom had a separate entrance on another road, a low door which scraped the floor. Inside full-sized men, perhaps twenty of them, sat on children's chairs at children's desks. Their awkwardness made it seem they had never sat on chairs before. Two paraffin lamps on table-tops threw big shadows everywhere, making it a problem for the hunched men to keep their paper in the light, to keep their hands, which overwhelmed stubs of pencils, from concealing what they wrote. The men were ragged; they smelled. At the front a younger man, a boy, clothes less torn and patched, hair less neglected, stood by a blackboard, chalk poised. At the sight of Fuller everything stopped.

Kamara smiled and talked, some of it in English, some not. He took Fuller's hand at one point as demonstration of their connection. Fuller caught the words 'aid', 'professor', 'economist', 'English'. There were a few questions, keen looks, brisk replies from Kamara.

'They are suspicious,' he reported proudly. 'They don't know why you should be here. Actually it is difficult to explain. This is good. I am happy at this. You see, these dockworkers do not just accept what I say. They question it. They insist on democracy. At one time they would just believe what I told them. And they would not question someone like you. No, they would have done anything you told them. This is what these classes are about. I hope you don't mind answering questions.' Kamara was enjoying himself.

They had been walking through the town in the evening, talking as they often did nowadays, Kamara's talk dancing between shy confidences and brisk boastfulness. Abruptly – he had been talking about the aunt who brought him up – Kamara said, 'Come, I want to show you something.' Now Fuller, shocked by the sudden attention of twenty pairs of eyes, suggested that perhaps it had been a mistake to bring him here: he did not want to intrude, some things were better kept quiet. He missed his table in the empty lounge of the Ambassador and he missed the passive fascination of hearing Kamara's monologues while they walked the twilight streets.

'No, no,' said Kamara, perhaps incapable of imagining that Fuller, so old, so big, so white, could be embarrassed, or perhaps impatient of Fuller's passivity and insisting on the danger of energy. 'It's interesting. You are here now. You have to stay. You can't run away. Anyway I want to see what they ask you.'

Kamara scattered provoking sentences to the group, got no reply, tried again, received a short speech from a man with one clouded eye, chuckled, translated for Fuller.

'Ah, all right. Now he wants to know if you have come here just to laugh at them or whether you are going to help them. He says they know they are not clever and cannot speak much English or write, so why should they have people like you come to look at them. I think he means it is humiliating. Then he says that if you want to help it is all right. They haven't got money for paraffin for their lights or for books and some of them haven't even got pencils and papers. What do you say to that?'

'You'd better say that I have not brought them anything. I came as your friend. At your invitation.'

'Ah, but they will not accept that. It ignores the social and economic differences between them and rich white people. How can you be a friend? What is your common interest? OK, I'll tell them what you said.'

Kamara spoke for several minutes before turning back to Fuller. 'I've been helping them analyse the question. I think it was a primitive response. If they think only of receiving favours from the rich they cannot progress. They will perpetuate their dependency. They have to claim economic power for themselves. I'll ask if they have any more questions.'

The men were quiet now, many of them staring at their desk tops. The boy who had been teaching had sat down, deferring to Kamara. Some of the men looked ill. In spite of the diversion of Fuller's visit two had slumped into sleep.

Kamara waited, then spoke again. 'I've told them that I've brought them an opportunity and that they should use it. All the time we talk about exploitation, how the rich and powerful exploit the poor. I've told them I have brought them someone who is from the rich and powerful, who advises governments and banks. This is their chance. If they want to know how the world works they should ask the powerful, not the powerless. I've told them that this is their chance to interrogate the enemy.' He laughed. 'I hope you don't mind. It's just pedagogy. You are a teaching aid.

'OK, now they are formulating some questions. Good. All right, they want to know about food. It's predictable. They want to know why, when they work so hard all day, they cannot afford enough to eat. One says his family is hungry. Another says his wife has left him and gone back to her village.'

Fuller explained, smiled and explained. Kangaba was poor; it could not afford to import much grain. If they imported more it would be cheaper, but if the price was lower the farmers of Kangaba would be discouraged from producing themselves. These were some of the problems.

The men looked blank, then one said, 'Mercedes Benz,' and the others laughed and echoed it, delighting Kamara.

'You see, they are making connections. We have been through this before. If no rice, how can the rich have Mercedes Benz? They understand it is a class thing.'

Everyone talked at once. Fuller heard in English: 'government', 'Uncle', 'Syrian', and, repeatedly, 'exploitation' – a word they seemed to love and which washed around the room like a magic incantation. Kamara smiled and let the noise rise. He shouted in Fuller's ear, 'You see, they don't accept your analysis, they have their own ideas. They are angry.'

The noise did seem angry. Not anger at Fuller, but an anger shared among themselves, a mutual indulgence in anger. Kamara, turning away from Fuller, topped the noise with a single phrase, clenching his fist above his head. The noise subsided; he repeated the phrase. This time there was an echoed response from the group. He repeated it a third time, with insistence, flexing at the knees. This time the response was strong and was followed by a conspicuous quiet. Kamara did not explain.

'OK, we'll be more organised. Sam, bring the posters. Hugh, you'll tell them if you agree with their analysis. This is how our literacy class works. They are learning to write in English. They want that. It's the language of power, of governments. First they start off by deciding what is most important to them. We don't use any old British textbooks. No! What have they got to do with a Kangaban dockworker – John and Mary visit the zoo, and so on? They always decide on a subject like dock work or rice or housing. These are what are important to them. Then we draw pictures. You see, there's rice coming off a ship. There's a woman cooking rice in her yard. There's a farmer. Everything to do with rice. Look over here at the later ones. There's a politician in his

Mercedes Benz. And there's the white man giving him money. They start with something essential like rice and learn the words that have to do with it. 'I eat rice'; 'Farmers grow rice' – things like that. Then as they think about what they write the picture gets bigger. They see that the problem of not being able to feed their families is not their fault, it's because of the actions of people far away. So they become keen to write. They want to describe their situation. At the same time they become more conscious. They have become more politicised. You cannot believe what I have seen in this room. These men felt helpless, now they can do something. My heart fills up when I think of it. All their lives these men have been treated as hardly better than animals. OK, they want to know what you think. Are they right in their analysis?'

Fuller hesitated, overwhelmed. He turned to the hand-drawn posters now spread everywhere around the room. The white man had a briefcase, a pointed nose, glasses. He was taller and fatter than the Africans. He was passing a wad of banknotes through the window of the car to a smiling Kangaban in a suit and tie. Thin figures, sweating painfully, pushed the car from behind.

After a pause Kamara whispered, 'You'd better tell them you agree.'

'I think,' said Fuller, 'that they have analysed the situation very well.'

Some nodded immediately, others waited for Kamara's translation before smiling their approval. There was a little light applause.

'OK, can we go?'

'I'm ready,' replied Fuller.

'Good. I must just ask them if they want to ask you more questions. It's fair I think . . . No, they are finished with you.' Without drawing breath Kamara again shouted a slogan, raised his fist, got a response, guided Fuller through the door. Outside he explained, as if embarrassed, 'I have to do some of that political shouting. They expect it.'

Away from the docks, walking through the quiet night-time streets, Fuller broke the silence. 'Latif, I don't think you should have shown me this. This is the sort of thing it is better to keep quiet. What use is it for me to know?'

After a further hundred yards, during which Fuller twice heard him sigh, Kamara replied. 'Actually you are right. It was not a professional thing to do. It was not good revolutionary practice. Sometimes I just get carried away.'

25

Regina, when they were in bed, after they had made love – this time Fuller taking the lead – was angry. She had met some old friends from the Sun and they had told her about Fatmata, the Fula girl who first introduced her to European men. While she told Fuller of her complaint she sat up in the bed, freed her hands from Fuller and talked to the wall, absorbed in her grievance.

'My sisters, they say that this girl meets an American at the Sun. It is only since a few weeks. It was the time I was meeting you. I have not been to the Sun since that time. After just four days this man takes Fatmata away. Four days! He doesn't even know what sort of girl this is. It's wonderful!' she added bitterly.

'So he takes her to his home in America and makes her his wife. Is true! No family, nothing. Now she is back with him for a holiday. He is an expert like you. This girl sits around the swimming pool where we cannot go and none of the boys at the hotel can say anything to her anymore. This is Fatmata. She is not a good girl at all. Honestly, that girl would go with anyone. She would do anything. She only thinks of the money. That American, he is very stupid. He does not even know her name is Fatmata. She calls herself Diana with foreigners. I tell you, if you meet this girl her legs just fall apart like this.' Regina pressed her forearms together then let her hands flop sideways. 'You would not like this girl, Hoo. Even if you meet her in public she will pull her breasts out of her dress like this.' She made a scooping motion. 'Yes! Even she will pull her dress up for you, just standing there. She is not a good girl. How can God smile on her like this. How can it be so? How can this girl be fortunate and not me?'

This time the tears burst, not seeping quietly, and Fuller thought he actually heard among her sobs and cries the sound 'boo-hoo', which he had never heard before. He took her in both arms but she pushed him away. He tried again, insisting on the strength of his large arms and this time she collapsed to him, causing Fuller the sharp pain of realisation that in doing nothing he had done this.

26

Dear Sheila,

I don't know whether you got my last letter or whether you read it if you did get it. I've a young friend here, Latif Kamara, who tells me that the clerks at the post office take the stamps off letters and resell them. That accounts for why you always have to use the post office glue-pot to stick the stamps on. If you did read it I hope it didn't upset you too much. I honestly don't know what effect my letters have on you. Perhaps you just think of me as a distant nuisance and don't pay any attention.

What I want to say is that I don't really feel badly about you. In fact I admire you. When I married you, you seemed not to have much ambition beyond being my wife and having my children. You were a good woman and I loved you. But now I see you were much more than that – I was blind not to see what else was in you. It is my fault that I didn't actively encourage you with your interests and a career. I was always away and preoccupied. But you've done marvellously in spite of me. You've made a lovely home and Melissa and Andrew are wonderful children. Then there's your work with the Samaritans and nuclear disarmament – that takes real courage and ability. I never entered your world fully – I was always up in the air concerned with nothing less than tens or hundreds of millions of dollars. I didn't set out to be that way – it seems that I was just claimed by that world and because of something in me I didn't resist. I never focused on small things. I suppose I couldn't see the trees for the woods. So, if you were, please don't be hurt by my last letter. It was just a passing mood and now I feel more balanced.

I seem to be getting a bit involved in Kangaba in spite of myself. It's a lovely country. The people have a way of talking to strangers as if they had known you all their lives. And there's an assumption that they understand everything that's important about everyone. They assume that people are attracted by sex and wealth, and that friends and family are important. After these things they don't seem to give much weight to anything else. I think they may be nearer to the truth than all our sophisticated thinkers. Still, they are affected by the outside world and politics and so on. I understand that in a new way. Latif, who I think I mentioned in my last letter, is a real idealist. He's young enough to be my son but even though he's an awkward cuss I can't help liking him. I fear, though, for any idealist in this situation. I know enough about such countries to know that this one could blow up at any time. Of course people like me are never affected. I've been in plenty of countries having unrest before.

I've no plans for leaving. I can't really see the point. I try not to think about work. Life is taking on a bit of a pattern. In some ways I feel more settled.

Love to Andrew and Melissa,

Look after yourself,

Love, Hugh

27

In Rome, four weeks before Kangaba, a woman attempting suicide fell noiselessly and horizontally – as if reclining – past Fuller's gaze. He moved to the window of the office to reassure himself that it had been a trick of the light, but she lay on the ground beneath him. Her only movement had been the slow reach of her hand to the hem of her skirt, trying to cover her thighs. In the empty seconds before people ran to her he tried to imagine that she had only tripped, that she was standing up, brushing herself down and walking on.

28

Jacob arrived brisk, Italian shoes tapping on the Ambassador's tiles, reaching Fuller quickly where he sat at his table, Fuller for the first time in a jacket – his beige lightweight linen – and a tie. It was for Jacob; Fuller had nothing to say.

'Your minister,' one of the girls at reception whispered loudly to another, who Jacob must have had.

'Hugh, are you ready? Uncle is expecting us.' Jacob looked at his thin, gold watch, looked at it again.

They took Jacob's best Mercedes, black, not blue, the latest model, the driver uniformed. 'No, Government House! Not the palace.' And Jacob turned from the driver to Fuller to report – just imagine – that the driver had wanted to take them to the wrong place. Jacob, sitting forward on the edge of the seat, giggled.

'You like my new car? All the ministers have new Mercedes now. Can you imagine? With the country bankrupt. But Uncle explained. He said the new Mercedes would save foreign exchange because they used less petrol than the old ones.' Jacob laughed, then hesitated, but finally could not resist. 'The only trouble is we've kept the old ones too . . . Ah, we are there.'

The journey had been two hundred yards – downhill. 'No, driver, the main gate, the one with the soldier. This is an official visit. Tha's right. My flag is flying? Good . . . No, we just drive past him – we don't have to explain ourselves. I'm a minister, isn't it? . . . All right, we better slow down now, let them see us. Please.'

Inside the gate, at which the single soldier had stamped a single foot in ceremony, a dozen young men lounged around the courtyard in exaggerated casualness, reclining on the steps, squatting under ornamental trees. One tight cluster was concentrating on a grey metallic object, perhaps a radio, perhaps plundered. Each wore, or displayed from an epaulette or pocket, a dusty red beret of the President's SDF. Their automatic rifles were trailed or cradled, or laid to rest within arm's reach, as if each young man owned a pet cat which he loved.

They slowly moved around the car, pressing unselfconscious faces to the tinted glass until Jacob opened an electric window and smiled an explanation.

'I'm a minister!' he hissed to Fuller as the window whined shut and a disfigured teenager waved them on. 'I hate all this.'

The President's secretary, a gracious young man in an embroidered white robe which Fuller judged expensive, led them through corridors which at first gave on to office doors but later had blank walls. 'In here, please.' He awkwardly held open one of a pair of high doors, arm straining, indicating that first Jacob, then Fuller and then himself should enter. 'His Excellency is waiting for you.'

The President was seated at the far end of a long windowless room. His high desk was wide and empty so that his sloping shoulders and boulder head rose like a small mountain relieving an immense plain. The visitors' chairs were fifteen feet from the President's desk and he made no movement to welcome them or offer his hand. Jacob moved his arm a fraction, warning Fuller that he should not approach; the secretary, retreating backwards, used both hands to indicate that they should sit, and then sat himself, discreet in the furthest corner. The four waited in silence. In front of Uncle was a thin cardboard file, the only interruption of the polished surface, but he ignored it, his eyes preferring a blanker spot to which they had been fixed since Fuller's entrance. Jacob ran his fingers down his tie. Fuller, a little put out, crossed his legs and then uncrossed them in the faintest protest.

When Uncle looked up his small eyes went directly from the desk to Jacob's face, not curious of Fuller. In the eyes was the dullest suggestion of a question and from the back of the room the secretary gave the meanest of nods.

Jacob stood. 'Your Excellency, thank you for meeting us. I have come as you suggested to introduce Mr Fuller to you. Mr Fuller is a very senior consultant economist who is visiting

Kangaba these days. His brief, among other things, is to advise the aid donors' meeting in December, which, as you will remember, will discuss Kangaba debt rescheduling. This, of course, as you know, is a very important meeting. Mr Fuller is also a very close old friend of mine. He was a very distinguished teacher at Oxford University when I was there. He helped me a lot in my study of Kangaban sectoral planning. You remember . . .' Uncle's eyes had made the journey from Jacob's face to Fuller's, moved, it seemed, by a slight wincing of impatience – hardly detectable, but enough to silence Jacob.

When he spoke there was the minimum of movement. His hands, so small compared to the wide face, did not make the slightest sympathetic gesture but remained relaxed on the desk top. Fuller wondered if he suffered from a respiratory illness in which the energy needed for even the tiniest movement had its cost. Or perhaps it was his heart. The voice was low, cracked and monotonic, the mouth seeming merely to release the sound rather than forming it. To make out the President's words from fifteen feet Fuller discovered that – to his irritation – he needed to strain forward in his chair.

'You are welcome to Kangaba, Mr Fuller. We are always pleased to have financial experts here to help us. We are in the hands of people like yourself. My minister says you are an influential man. If you say we use our money well the banks will give us more. If you say the President puts the money in his Swiss bank accounts maybe they will not. Maybe they will say we should punish that senile old man, we've had enough of him. It's not easy to run Kangaba. My people want to split into bits and pieces. I am a simple man. I hardly read and write. But without me, what is Kangaba? If there is no money I cannot feed my people. They will starve. They will fight in the streets. Already my own people are attacking my home. There are troublemakers. I believe you know that. What should I do? You are an expert. Perhaps I will ask you to advise me. I will have to sacrifice. To keep my head I will have to lose my arms and legs. I will have to fight my own people in the streets. Maybe even I will have to give up my ministers.' He stopped and as Fuller watched his face distorted, the cheeks gathered as if clawed back by invisible hands and from somewhere deep a single bubble of laughter rose to escape, like marsh gas.

'If you want to stay, you can stay. We have easy ways. You can help us with the IMF. When you are a small animal you have to get along with bigger animals. This is what I told your queen at her daughter's wedding. They say she is a hunter. Cesay, you can give him what he wants. The Libyan house on the beach if you like. It's empty. I didn't like the Libyans.'

Tiredness and bad temper seemed to overtake him simultaneously as if the effects of a drug had suddenly worn off. His eyes slid back to the desk top and his hand made a small dismissive movement of distaste indicating that he had been drawn into an excessive civility. The secretary was quickly on his feet, guiding the visitors to the door, and when Fuller turned, expecting to catch Uncle's eye, still willing, through habit, to offer some expression of thanks, he found the President otherwise absorbed, making some tiny adjustment to an inconspicuous badge affixed to his oddly narrow lapel.

Outside, in the car, when they had passed through the gate, Jacob turned to Fuller. 'You heard that! You heard that! It was a threat. Yes. I think so. You see! . . . Driver, please, down the side road, please. And stop.' Jacob pushed open the door and vomited into the ditch, yellow flecks clinging to the car's black paintwork.

By the time they reached the hotel entrance Jacob was once more composed. 'I'm sorry, Hugh. I don't like you to see me like this. I expect I am imagining things. I need a holiday. You can just forget this meeting if you like. You have to do your job. You're in a different world from me. That is my confusion.'

29

Palace Puzzle – Is Our President Safe?

The VIP residents of Braithwaite Heights were alarmed by gunfire in the night last week coming from the direction of their neighbour in the Presidential Palace. We are told that nothing is wrong but as loyal citizens we are worried for Uncle's safety. Our informants tell us that at eleven pm Tuesday they heard gunfire from the palace and soon after the floodlights on the perimeter fence went out. Gunfire continued sporadically for over one hour. There has been no official word on the incident and we cannot believe the rumours that it was the President's own Special Defence Force which attacked his home. Even if they have not been paid it is no excuse to plunder the President's palace at the point of a gun. If Uncle cannot trust the SDF who is left?

And *Flash* asks, what are the British doing here with the SDF? Every year we see the British army playing games on our soil under the excuse of training our fighting men. Uncle tells us we should be grateful but we ask him not to trust our old colonial masters too much. Does he know what the mysterious Colonel Watson and his men are doing with the SDF in the distant north of Kangaba? Loyal citizens need reassurance that their leader is master of his house.

Flash, September 15th

30

'The truth is I need to talk to someone like you.'

Fuller and Kamara were at the beach. Kamara had said, 'I'll take you to the beach. White people like beaches.'

'I've been thinking about what you said. I shouldn't trust you. That's true. It's not even that you might betray us. I don't believe that actually. I should not talk to anyone unnecessarily. I know that. But honestly, Hugh, sometimes I don't trust myself. Everyone comes to me for answers. They think I understand what is happening, but sometimes I just lie awake and wonder if I've got it all wrong. I've hardly been out of Kangaba all my life. Maybe there is some piece of knowledge I've missed just because no one told me it existed. I read quickly but you can hardly get books here. I have one "A" level GCE, that's as far as my education goes. But then I think, education isn't everything. Look at your friend with his doctorate, my minister. What does he understand? And if he understands, what does he do? He's a useless man. I'm sorry, I have to say that: he is useless. At least I can talk to you. I don't get the chance to talk to people at your level. That's why I am reckless with you. What I know of the international political economy is all theory, but you have been there. You know the world. If there is something big I don't know about which changes everything, you are the only one who can tell me. I've got no teacher, not even a father. My aunt took care of me. I will introduce you to my aunt. I want to do that.'

The empty beach was a perfect curve: white sand, blue sea. The sea seemed calm, yet far out it reared up into high, glassy waves which moved upright towards the beach, teetering but somehow keeping their balance until they were nearly at the shore, then bowing gracefully to gravity. On the beach all was order and regularity. Kamara and Fuller walked in step, Fuller in his sandals, Kamara still in his battered high-heeled boots.

'I came to Kingston when I was four. About four. My father is a trader who moves around and when my mother died in child-birth he sent me south to stay with my aunt. I hardly see him. In fact I do not even know what country he is in these days. My aunt is my real family. I think she is the only one I love, actually. Yes, I think so. I respect that woman so much.'

'In fact I don't have a girlfriend,' said Kamara, answering a question Fuller had not asked. They had stopped to watch the waves, each more with himself than with the other. 'I don't have time for that. I want to keep myself strong.' He paused and they turned to walk on in silence until Kamara seemed to find a new question in his own answer. 'I think sex makes you weak actually. I see these boys just filling their time with fucking – they just lie around all day. Somehow it doesn't weaken the girls, I don't know why. I think they take the man's strength. They are always coming to me. There are many girls who want to be my fuck-mate. Many, many girls. I tell you! They even send their brothers to request for me. But I always say no. They can't understand this. Some-times they make fun of me. Yes, that happens. These rough girls call out to me sometimes and say I just can't do it. But they don't abuse me too much actually because they respect me. I think so.'

Again Kamara fell silent but the sound of the sea seemed to induce from him a flow of confidences. 'I try to keep myself strong. I have some chest expanders under my bed and I use them every day when I get up and before I go to bed. I never sleep more than five hours. I don't need more sleep than that. I don't think anyone needs more than that. If I just keep moving around I don't get tired. I can push on. Even if I miss a whole night I can go through the next day. When I am tired I can just sleep on the ground or on a bench like a poor person. I have to be able to do that. If you are serious you have to be able to do without comforts or you are dependent. It is that which makes you bourgeois. In the north, near the desert, the Fula nomads can go for days and days without eating. I've seen that. I respect them for that. I have tried myself but I get weak. The rural people, the peasants and nomads, are really strong. They will win in the end because they are not dependent. I've learned this from my family village in the north. I can still trace my family there. Sometimes I go and stay there. I have to learn what it is like to be a peasant – I am very ignorant in that direction. I confess that. You should see this village, Hugh. The people there had one of your foreign aid projects.

'Sometimes I am lonely. I should say that. I have many comrades of course. I think I can trust them. You see how when I walk through Kingston everybody greets me. But sometimes I feel alone. It is true I would like a wife or a girlfriend. I sometimes think that. But I think it is not practical. Actually I read every night, so how can I share my bed with someone? It would not be fair. In any case Kangaba is dangerous these days, I should not involve anyone else in my life.

'In fact something strange always happens with girls. Even if they are beautiful they just turn into sisters. It confuses me actually. I tried when I was younger. When I was a schoolboy everyone had to do it. Of course there were girls. But I treated them as friends. They were always troubling me for this and that. They felt insulted if I did not want to go with them. I said it was better if men and women respected each other. You know, I used to argue with them so I didn't have to go with them. It was ridiculous actually. I would point at their friends who had to leave school because they were pregnant and I would try to convince them that there were better things to do with their time. But they would never understand what I said. They even said they did not mind if they got pregnant – that they would like a baby. Honestly, these girls are foolish. They can't see ahead. They have no analysis, no sense of reality. Sometimes I would just do it to keep them happy, but I would not want to see them again. It has been a problem actually. Nobody here thinks as I think about this. I can see you don't think as I think either. You have Regina. I think it is all right. Yes, I think so. Regina has had bad luck, actually. In fact no young man here would want to marry her now. No, I don't think they would. She is lucky to have someone like you. I do not think she has had someone like you before.

'Actually I do have some women friends. Some of my best friends – comrades actually – are women. I trust them. But there is nothing else between us. It is my fault. I just hold back. I can only think of my strength. It's true! Strength to do my work. I must be ready to kill if necessary. I have prepared my mind for that. Not everyone likes me for this. They think I am not like them, that I am aloof. But it's just the way it is. These women become my sisters. I can only be friends with them that way. What do you think, Hugh? Is it good to be like this?'

31

Fuller was a backstreet child. Their Nottingham terrace house opened directly on to a narrow street; his mother blancoed the front step daily, accepting the footprints of the less fastidious without protest. It was simply that the standards must be kept. He remembered how the step was wavy with wear, how comfortable it was for a small boy in short trousers on a summer day, hoping for war-planes in the sky.

In those days his father had been alive but untraceable. Mother wouldn't talk. Other children's fathers left for the war and then returned. Fuller's was not there before and did not come back afterwards.

It was a quiet childhood; he was not allowed to play ball games in the street with the other boys. His mother feared he would be lost, as perhaps his father had been lost, to haplessness, settling for the common round, and young Hugh, even as a child the man of the house, played his part. She always made clear that their poverty was one of circumstance, not because they belonged with the poor. After school, home closed around him, keeping him mysterious to the other boys. He made his own tea – and his mother's – when he returned from school and waited for her return. She arrived back from her clerk's job, stiff with dignity from the walk past the gossiping neighbours – fat and knowing in their aprons and head-scarves – and for a time she was quiet, as if talk might make her cry, before saying softly, perhaps giving him a quick hug, 'Put the kettle on now, Hugh. We'll read afterwards.'

There were books and the wireless. Their furniture was polished and of better quality than that of the neighbours. Somewhere, his mother implied, there were relatives of quality who would, because of her pride, remain strangers. She would not talk of Fuller's father: he was not worth talking about.

At school, a scholarship boy, he did not naturally belong with the boys from the wealthier families, but neither did he keep up with the neighbourhood playmates who went to a different school. In spite of his reserve he was never bullied at school, not only because he was big but because there was in his quietness something contained which was respected. The supporting evidence of depth came in spurts, such as a seemingly effortless superiority in mathematics in the year it first became difficult, which was reined back to merely average in the following year. At one time he took up the javelin and, with a technique all his own, claimed the school record before losing interest. There was nothing assertive about these achievements; if anything he was embarrassed by their failure to conform with his accepted status.

His mother died, still in the same house, still hoping for a better future, when Fuller was twenty-three. It was cancer; it didn't last long. Fuller was left with a university degree, his mother's ambitions, and an abiding anger that she had never been given a life that matched her intelligence and character.

32

'Ah . . . these girls, why don't they leave me alone? Frances, why are you here? No, it's not right. You can't just turn up at my home when you feel like it. You see, Hugh, I get no rest. Ali! Aleee! Where is that boy? He is supposed to look after the house, but where is he? He's a relative. It's worse – they think you owe them something. He steals my shirts and his family just thinks it's all right. No . . . Please, Hugh take a seat. We'll have a drink. Aleee! You see these girls? They just arrive on my doorstep in a taxi and wait for me. They know I am weak. No Frances, you must go. We have serious things to talk about – Mr Fuller is from England. He's an important man – we don't want women around us. He's still a young man isn't he? Yes, good. Anyway you must go; he doesn't need you either. I'll give you the money for a taxi. You have to rotate these girls, Hugh. They get presumptuous. It is time this one is rotated. Please leave us now. Just go. Please! Ah good, here's the boy. Why were you not here? What sort of nonsense is this? I bring VIPs home and I can't even offer them a drink because you are off somewhere with your little personal business – I don't know what. No, I don't care. Please just bring the drinks. Why are you standing? Ah, all right, here's the key to the cupboard – the little key. And bring it straight back to me . . . And open the windows – and the doors. It's too hot in here. No, not now. We need the drinks. And bring the tables over to our chairs. Do I have to tell you everything each time? No, the drinks, first the drinks. And ice . . . Relax, Hugh, please. This is my house. Relax. You can see the bay from here.'

Jacob leaned back on one of the velour sofas. Although it was the early evening cool the new lines on his forehead were brimming with sweat. His eyes were dreadfully bloodshot. While Fuller settled in a comfortable easy chair and took in the costly furnishing – undisciplined by any common style – Jacob took off his jacket, unbuttoned his waistcoat to set free his childish paunch, discarded his shoes, socks, tie and rolled his trousers to his knees. 'Ah, Hugh, it's terrible.'

'I dream of Oxford. Philosophy . . . Schiller . . . Schopenhauer . . . That linguistics man – you see, I've forgotten. Do you see any books in this room? No, they are in boxes somewhere. Sometimes I think of our time together in Oxford. The dinner parties – you were brilliant, Hugh. You never said much but we all listened to you. I always talked too much. The debates – I loved debating. I miss all that here. Who is there to talk to? Sometimes I have talked to you in my mind. I mean it! I have imagined how you would have analysed the situation here – I'm so buried in it I can't see. Please have a drink. Give Mr Fuller a whisky. With ice. Leave a bottle with him. And the table . . . how can he reach it there? Move the table to him. No, not with the drinks on, you will break everything. Ah, it's hopeless, Hugh. You see, even the simplest thing I have to supervise. I am supposed to make a national development plan – can you imagine? Who is going to execute it? It's you people who want things like national plans. You don't understand. You know I can do it, Hugh – that's not the problem. You know my doctoral thesis.

'No, I am happy you are here. I can talk seriously with you, I don't have to pretend. I have a difficult job, Hugh. You mustn't be hard on us. We are a poor country – just victims. Still you all want repayment of your loans . . . You must help me.' Jacob seemed preoccupied, the words automatic. He poured himself another glass of whisky and pushed away a puppy with his foot – not harshly.

'I had another dog once – you know my wife stays with her family in the north these days. It was just a yellow bush dog. The neighbours poisoned it. I don't know why.'

'I didn't want to go into politics. You know I didn't. I just wanted to be an academic – or maybe an international civil servant.

Uncle made me stand for election – before he stopped the elections. He drove my campaign himself – we used to call him the campaign driver. It was horrible. You know no one gets into parliament without someone getting killed. Someone always has to be killed.' Jacob's eyes, which had been averted, slid to Fuller's then away. Fuller did not press him.

'You see, we can't say no. I thought I might be able to make something out of being an MP after all. I was so conceited about my Oxford doctorate. I thought I was as clever as Uncle. He's a crude man; you've seen him.' Jacob drank the glass of whisky as if it were beer and poured himself another. He laughed a sharp ironic laugh, his face dripping sweat. He fidgeted on the sofa, somehow unable to find a comfortable position. 'Last year nobody was paid. Not the MPs, not even the ministers. Uncle made a speech. He said that any politician who could not make a good income from his job did not deserve the position. He said that if we couldn't look after ourselves, how could we look after the country? It's crazy – he turns everything upside down. It gives a person such a headache being in this place. I loved logical argument, you know that. Those debates. Now where is the logic? It's like going through the looking glass. My head spins. Imagine, Hugh! We have to be corrupt to serve our country! That's his logic!' Again Jacob laughed. The sweat made it seem he was crying through every pore.

'It was horrible. I was trying – honestly Hugh I remembered what you taught me, what we discussed. This is a poor country. It's a beautiful country. I wanted to do something. But you people do not understand. You make some new agreement and you don't know what it costs. Uncle has told me I am not corrupt enough. He called me to his office and said he had given me one of the best ministries – Economic Affairs. He said he couldn't understand how I could deal with the IMF, the international banks, foreign firms without getting rich. He didn't like it. He scared me. Again now he has made me scared. He told me I should have a bigger house. Look at this house – I have twelve rooms just for myself. No, I should have a house next to his palace on the hill over there. He said he was going to sell me the land for a hundred thousand dollars. I couldn't refuse; I had to find the money. I will not tell you how I found the money, Hugh. I am too ashamed. Please never tell anyone in Oxford any of this. I just have to tell you – it's sending me crazy, you being here. I love you actually, Hugh. You were a real friend, not a friend for money. I know what you did for me in Oxford. It's like Oxford has come to Kangaba. I cannot be in both places at the same time. It's sending me crazy . . . Yes, I was telling you, this new house. I found the money. Uncle has already sent me the contractors I have to use. You know where the house is going to be? Look. You see the palace up there on that empty hill? The new road going up to it? The floodlights and below them the wire fencing. That's where my new house is going to be – just in front of the palace. The palace has been attacked three times already. I will be the first line of defence. Anyone attacking the President will kill me first. He is brilliant. How could I ever think I was clever enough to deal with him? I've paid a hundred thousand dollars to be sentenced to death!' Jacob's laugh went high until it seemed to choke him. 'Excuse me, an ulcer. I'm going to vomit. Excuse me.' He stumbled from the room.

When Jacob returned a minute later his face was towelled dry, the shine replaced by a dull greyness. 'Please Hugh, I want you to help me. I don't know how. Maybe you can write something in your report . . . If the aid donors are tough on us now, Uncle will blame me. He doesn't understand about ideas. He calls the country socialist. Imagine! I don't even know where he found the word. He only understands that you are my friend and that you have some power. We need our loans extended – rescheduled. You often do it I know. The donors will listen to you. Look I'll give you all the figures. Everything is open to you. No secrets. I'll send everything to you – I'll give it to Kamara. I can't even look at figures any more. Economic affairs! It's a joke. Try, Hugh – I know you can do something. You leave Kangaba but I have to stay. My family, you see . . . At least don't go away for a while – if you are here I am safe. I know that. Oh God, Hugh, I dream of Oxford. It was heaven. I dream of it.'

33

We Are Not Subversives

Our readers have the right to know that *Flash* did not appear last week through no fault of its own. Un-uniformed thugs attacked our press, beat our typesetter and arrested our editor who languishes even now in the Valley Prison. But we are back! We live by our motto: 'The truth will out!'

Your Excellency The President, we the humble journalists of *Flash* wish to assure you that our loyalty to Kangaba is not in doubt. Those who may wish to mislead you by calling us subversives do not know what they are talking about. They are political ignoramuses who do not even know the meaning of the words they use. A subversive is someone who wishes to undermine the security of the state, but our wish is only to serve. The President is the embodiment of Kangaba and it is our duty as journalists to point out when those who act in your name do not seem to act in your interest. If we breached sensitive matters of national defence by asking about the SDF and their British advisers, our only fault was excessive zeal in our concern for Kangaba and yourself as its leader.

The Proprietors

Flash, September 22nd

34

'This is my aunt. She is seventy, maybe eighty. Nobody knows for sure.'

The old lady bent from her hips to capture a fallen garment with her fingertips, then held the moment, enforcing a proper pause before she slowly straightened to stand before Fuller. She was slender, tall and made taller by an intricately arranged headscarf of a cloth that matched her wrapper. Fuller looked then looked again and saw that, yes, its pattern was made up of portraits of the English queen. Seeing Fuller seeing this, Kamara's aunt slowly smiled and the crinkled face became only its even lips and teeth and its high round cheeks – a smile of such immense womanly charm that, shockingly, Fuller imagined he might fall in love. Her eyes, above all this, were clear.

She spoke, Kamara translated. 'She says you are welcome. She says that I am a son to her and that if you are my friend then you also must be hers.'

But first Fuller must be comfortable; he must sit in the armchair. Latif too, her nephew, must be seated. She, herself, sat up against the edge of the bed that dominated her room, a bed so high with its several mattresses and giant brass frame that even sitting she was almost standing. Beneath it, trunks and treasures were tight-packed and it was from one of these, while Fuller waited, that she took a twisted cloth and, from that, extracted coins. A child was called and Kamara said to Fuller that he would take a soft drink wouldn't he, and Fuller said he would. The money was counted, the child sent on his way. 'She says she wishes to speak to you. No, it's a more formal word. There's no real translation actually. She wishes to address you. I think that's better.'

She had a small, compelling voice which made the language seem like birdsong. Her hands, too, flew, long fingers curved backwards, shaping meaning in brief flights. She spoke with perfect composure and, after the first few sentences, with obvious fluency, engaging Fuller's eyes in a way that Moslem women should not and perhaps only Moslem women can. While Kamara translated she held the bond with a still smile and Fuller felt again the confusion of being drawn into an intimacy of charm with a woman of seventy, maybe eighty.

'She says that these days there is a heaviness on her heart. There are serious problems in Kangaba. All her life she has worked as a market woman but she never thought to see what she has seen these days. I think she means the killing of the market women. She is their leader. You know about that. She says she has brought up a family' – Kamara chuckled – 'She says it was a big family and very difficult with relatives like me. All this time she has managed. She has lived with the English. For their own reasons they came and for their own reasons they left. When they left we made Kangaba and for a time we were happy. She says she prospered. Actually she says more than that. She says we had good food, she built a house, the children all went to school and when they were old enough everyone could afford to be married. She says that I am the exception, the troublesome one. Actually I am her favourite.

'But now things are bad. She does not know why. She is an old lady. She is being modest, I think. She says she can remember when there was plenty of rice. People came from other parts of West Africa to buy rice in Kingston. She had only to sit here and her relatives from the villages brought rice to her. She paid them or perhaps she sent their children to school in Kingston for them, and she sold the rice in the market. She was happy. They were happy. Things were as they should be. This was a long time since. Now the rice does not come from the villages. She has to go and look for rice. And nowadays she cannot even find it; she has to buy imported rice from the government-licensed importers. But they will not sell to her at the official price so how can she afford to buy it? All the Syrians and Indians are hoarding the rice because they expect a government price rise. Now she wants to tell you what this means to Kangabans. She says you are English

– I think you know that – and for you life is different. You eat all sorts of things – potatoes, she says, bread – but Kangabans have to eat rice. Rice is all they need. Rice is all they want. It's true, what she says. There's a saying here: If you haven't eaten rice, you haven't eaten.

'Now she says she wants to tell you the story of her life. She says it is a story of rice. I hope you are not bored.' Fuller said he wasn't bored, absolutely not. 'She says she wants you to understand. In these days perhaps you are the sort of man who can help us.

'She was born in the village of Dubeng in the north of the country. When she was thirteen she married a Mandinka rice trader from another place. She says her family was not happy. She could have had any man. Her breasts were like so, her bottom like so.' Kamara laughed as his aunt's hands soared and dived around her teenage shape. Her smile held Fuller. 'The family said that a stranger would mistreat her, the women in his family would humiliate her and soon she would ask for her brothers to come and fetch her and her dowry back home. But even in those days she was stubborn and had her own mind.

'Her husband took her to Kingston and for a time they were happy and prosperous until her husband fell sick with fevers. She says he was already quite an old man – actually, I think he was in his forties. She had to do everything for him. She did the trading, she bought medicines from the government dispensaries – it seems we had dispensaries in those days – and from the local healers. She went to the Moslem marabouts and bought charms and prayers. She did everything to stop her husband dying. But she could not help because her husband's competitors were jealous of his business and his young wife and had bought powerful prayers for her husband's death.' Kamara paused, then turned to Fuller. 'This will seem strange to you but she believes it completely. Everyone believes it here. Even I cannot explain everything that happens.' Fuller nodded back to say he had an open mind. 'She says that when her husband died, the men who did it came to claim her and her children but she cursed their ancestors and took over her husband's business herself. She swore that never again would she depend on a man. She thinks she was nineteen when this happened.

'She struggled to become a successful trader in her own right. Her home village sent her rice and vegetables when they could and she helped the villagers when they travelled to Kingston. Her house was always full. Even today she has twenty people staying with her. I think that's an exaggeration, but anyway she's right, her home is always full. She says she made journeys to other countries to buy and sell and always she looked after other people. She was without a man all this time but in her middle years she found a young man. She says he was beautiful – handsome – and that she herself was told that at that age she was still beautiful.'

It was, Kamara's aunt explained, England that had spoiled her happiness this time. England was fighting 'World War Two' – she used the English words – and they came and took her young man for the British army. By then she had enough money and she hoped for happiness too, but it was not to be. She never heard from her lover again. After many visits to the colonial government she was finally told that he was dead. He had died in a place called Burma, of which she had never heard. She dreamed of this Burma, but it was so far away she could not imagine it. Then she heard from a soldier who had returned that Burma was a 'place full of rice', which seemed a sort of paradise and she was able to sleep again. Much later – it was the time rice was becoming short in Kangaba, when Kamara had come to live with her and was going to school – she visited a remote village in the east of the country and found it full of rice. The farmers there were very clever, growing rice in the swamps and transplanting it – something unknown in Kangaba where they scatter rice. Her hands at this point flew left and right in demonstration and Fuller looked to her fingertips, expecting grains of rice to appear from them. She had asked about their rice and they told her that the method had been taught to them by an army veteran – now dead – who had learned of it during his stay in Burma. Her feelings about her love dying in a bright green paradise were confirmed but she kept the knowledge to herself – she didn't want the other traders to know about her new rice supply.

Her only unease in this vision of the place of her lover's death was the absence of people. She had been told they were not Africans but it seemed they also were not Syrians, Indians or Europeans, which exhausted her knowledge of human types. Only when Kung Fu films arrived in Kingston – she was the only old lady in the cinema – did she find, in the Chinese, a race which seemed to fill the picture. Burma was a paradise of brilliant green rice and dazzling acrobatic jinn. Her lover had been claimed by a holy and magical place.

At this point Kamara's aunt had paused and the smile that she rested on Fuller said, in a complicated way, I know it's only a story, I admit I'm only charming you. Kamara said, 'We all know this story. She likes to tell it. Maybe it's true.'

'It is true,' enunciated his aunt in careful English.

'Oh, I should have said,' Kamara added with a laugh. 'She knows some English. Only a few words I think.' His aunt nodded with mock gravity and reached again beneath her bed to find a bottle opener for the little girl, who had waited patiently, clasping two bottles of Fanta and a palmful of change.

Kamara's aunt did not take a drink herself but watched her guests each take a draught before she continued. The room was hotter than when they had arrived; the evening cool would be slow to penetrate it.

'OK, now she is saying again that the old ways are upside down these days. Instead of people in the village sending her rice, she has to send them rice from the town because they are hungry too. She asks, how can this be? How can we be sending rice from where we don't grow it to where we grow it? Some people say that the village people are lazy but she has thought about it and does not see it that way. Good! I'm happy to hear this. I have never heard my aunt talk like this before. She is very intelligent, I think. Listen! She says it is not that they are lazy but that all the young people are leaving the villages and there are only old people there to grow the rice. It is not their fault. There is nothing in the villages for them – no schools, no jobs – and the government presses very hard for its taxes. Where are the people going to find money for taxes in the villages? Growing rice and eating it does not bring money.

'These days it is even worse. Now we cannot even get rice for ourselves in the town and there is none for the villages. She says the rice comes in on boats. Some people even say that it is given free to Kangaba, but the licensed importers are hiding it until the government price goes up. She is asking how the government can put the price up when a family cannot even afford to buy one bag a month at the old price. I don't think you have to answer her. It's rhetorical. She says Kangaba cannot live like this. They want to do something but even when she and the other market women went to petition the President they were beaten by thugs. She is showing you how they were hit. Two were killed, two women – it was in the papers. This was the first time in her life she has seen this. What are they to do? Some people say foreigners are behind the price rise. Maybe you can explain it to her. Ah, now she says she does not sleep anymore because I am out on the streets.' He laughed lightly at the old lady's foolishness. 'She says she has known me since I was small – that is true, I came here when I was four. She says she paid for my school fees. I was always in mischief, but I was always top of my class. This is an old woman's talk – never mind it. Now she says I am making trouble and she can't blame me for it. She is scared for me but what can she say when her own sisters are being killed? Ah – this is interesting – she says I am a radio, I talk too much and too loud. She says a radio can never know who is listening. All her life, she says, she has respected the law. Her measures are always fair. She bought a market trader's licence even when the British were here and the others were avoiding it. But now she is scared that I will go to prison. Even that she will go to prison herself. When she should be resting as an old lady. Even, she is scared that one of us might be killed. So, she is asking for your help. She says that maybe you are the sort of man who can help us. You are up there and we are down here – that's the way she sees it. White people come and go, she says she knows that. It is only right that they should. They have their own homes. She says she knows that you must have a wife and children far away. You would not be a man if you did not. But she thinks you can talk to the big men who decide things. You know ministers, you know foreigners, even the President. Maybe because you are here in her house and you are my friend you are a little bit part of her family and you will not forget us. She says that perhaps if you do something I will not be on the streets being a radio.

'All right, she is coming to an end now. She doesn't want you to make promises. She knows you are only a man and what man promises Allah can overrule – that's a formality, everyone says that here. So she is grateful for your patience in listening to her. I think it has been interesting for you, actually. It's good for you to hear how ordinary people think.'

Fuller said he had required no patience, what she said had fascinated him, he had forgotten time listening to her voice. For a moment, during which all three were silent, he thought to answer her questions. He knew answers, had known them. He remembered it was wise to raise the price of rice, good economics, sound practice. It encouraged farmers. Fuller, in a lightweight suit, had argued it before. He wasn't the man to say it now; it would die on his tongue. Kamara was right, the poor would lose. He pushed himself up from the armchair and found that, after all, he was taller than the old lady, even with her headscarf. He took her slender hand. On the inside it was rough, on the outside it was wrapped in the finest, oldest skin. He thanked her again, told her of her charm, and walked with Kamara to the doorway, where, behind the curtain, he was surprised to discover it was still bright day.

35

Will J.C. Have To Go?

Rumour has it that our man in Economic Affairs has fallen out with his President. His crime is no greater than to ask our Syrian friends to live by the same laws as the rest of us humble citizens and not send all our money overseas. Poor J.C. looked into the Central Bank cupboard and didn't find enough Kangas to paper the shelves. But Uncle doesn't share J.C.'s views. With his greater wisdom he has pointed out that the Syrians create Kangaba's wealth and should be rewarded. Is it the fault of the Syrians that we Kangabans are so useless at business? Now J.C. will need his fancy Oxford doctorate if he is to keep his hot seat without getting burnt. With the Syrians angry, the people short of rice, the IMF vultures wanting their money and Uncle sitting on the fence, where can J.C. go? We watch with interest and you can be assured that *Flash* will be the first to tell you.

Flash, September 29th

36

'Hoo, you will reach my house today. I know you will. I am shamed for you to see it but it hurts my mind that you do not come to my house. I think about how you should meet my family. I should cook you food but we have only a small outside fire. I am ashamed. I dream of cooking you a meal on a big plate, a meal for a man of your size. I want to watch you while you eat. It is right isn't it? I know these things. I know how to please a man. Only it is that my family is poor, our house has been stolen from us. All my friends and family say, "Where is this man? Why do you not bring him to see us?" They say you must be too proud to sit with poor people. Or they say you do not exist and that my head has been confused to make up such stories. They want to know how it is I am not rich if I am loving a European man. I do not know how to answer these questions so I just keep quiet. In my mind I know you are a good man and that you love me. You are generous but you do not even think of money.'

While she talked, Regina dressed: the sensible pants, the bra, the lemon and blue polka-dot dress with flounces at the shoulders – the coarse stitching taking nothing from its generous curves and swirls. She stood up, placed her feet apart and, with head bowed in front of the mirror, ravaged her curls with a long-toothed comb. The movement was vigorous, almost angry, but her voice stayed small. Fuller was used to finding tiny black watch-spring curls in his cup or glass, had come to expect them, even want them. It was the nearest they had got to domesticity.

'I think it is right that you visit my home, isn't it? I know you have a European wife but where is she? I think she is an old lady. You said she is nearly your age isn't it? You are still a young man but for a woman it is not so young. I think she is past the age for loving you. She has her children. This is your European wife. Sometimes I am jealous of this woman though I do not know her. Then I think that she is there and you are here and by now she is old. You are in Kangaba. You will stay here. I know that. I know it in my heart. You cannot avoid loving me. I can see that. Perhaps you do not know it. You are still a stranger here, your head is not yet completely arrived in Kangaba. Yes, I think so. Men never know about loving. They think they do not need it. They think it is weak but in the end they discover that they cannot do without it.'

She came to Fuller, eyes bright, convinced by her own words, and bent towards where he lay on the bed, still naked, offering him the top of her head. 'You see my hair?' It was shiny, even, soft, tickling to the touch, and Fuller, obedient to the invitation, passed his hand lightly across it, his palm tingling. 'You see!' said Regina, her private thesis proved. 'You are loving me.' She brushed her hair across his chest and stomach and looked up at him with the eyes of a submerging seal as she slid between his legs. 'You like this?' Fuller half laughed, half groaned. 'I know you will reach my house today, Hoo. I know it.'

Fuller supposed there must have been a Lord Talbot who gave his name to Talbot Street. There was evidence that at some time the street had been part of a colonial plan for downtown Kingston. There had once been a tarred road, deep concrete storm drains and a raised pavement. Now pieces of concrete jagged at odd angles – no place for a blind man – and fragments had been removed and incorporated into the houses, which ranged from ornate two-storey homes to shacks of cardboard and scrap-metal. Flimsy roofs were held in place by the weight of stones mined from the road, which had been turned into a pitted moonscape. A heavy-duty Victorian street nameplate survived and there was a single traffic sign – the stylised flaming torch the British used to use to mark school crossings. The school and the traffic had gone. On the corner a red cast-iron post box stood as a further memorial to early colonial optimism, although only the simple-minded could confuse it with a place for posting letters – Talbot

Street denied such formality. Fuller took it all in while Regina bent to remove her shoes for the final fifty yards.

Regina's house was a poor place, a lean-to shack resting against a tumble-down house. The walls of the single room shack were made from oil drums beaten flat, a mode of construction not permitting windows. Outside, where Regina gestured Fuller to wait, was a little fenced courtyard with the clutter of recent cooking and laundry.

'Is that your house?' asked Fuller, pointing to the larger building, remembering her story. Regina shrugged and looked a little cross, as if sympathy was a cruel thing, and busied herself with sending small boys on errands. 'Give me two sticks,' she ordered Fuller and patted the cigarettes in his shirt pocket. These were sent off in the hands of the boys. Finally she relaxed from the job of organisation which had required her concentration and pulled back the curtain which hung across the shack's doorway. 'Go in. Go in.'

Inside was dark. The only light came from a small hole high up on the inside wall, which seemed to open into the larger house. It was barred, though it was too small for even a child to wriggle through. On the far sill a cheap radio played music, serving both households in a cooperative arrangement which seemed to contradict Regina's story of hostility. Fuller sat on a bed where Regina guided him, leaned back then leaned forward as his hand touched a damp tangle of sleeping children. A hand sought his and Regina said it belonged to her senior sister.

Fuller's eyes adjusted to the dark. The sister sitting to his left had a sluttish look, her hair tied into rough spikes and a threadbare wrapper worn loose over a capacious, grubby brassière. She was smoking one of Fuller's cigarettes. There were three children on the bed, two of them light enough to be mixed blood, and on the floor two light patches which caught Fuller's attention turned out to be the soles of the feet of a fourth child. Fuller could have stepped on them and broken the fragile ankles. 'Is this your son?' asked Fuller of Regina.

'No. This is my son,' and she shook awake one of the pale children on the bed. Her sister laughed in a hard way.

'No, don't wake him,' said Fuller. The child rubbed his eyes, took in Fuller, then dived back into the other warm bodies.

They sat on the edge of the bed, Regina, in the middle, quiet and neat in her pretty dress and high-heeled shoes, her sister also quiet, one hand resting inside her brassière. Fuller had tried to make conversation but the responses had been short. 'Shall we go?' he asked Regina quietly.

'No, you must stay.' She seemed shocked, puzzling Fuller.

The family arrived in the course of the next half-hour, perhaps following an elaborate system of precedents which, nevertheless, seemed imperfectly understood. Mostly it was women and children although sometimes a man would look in, as if checking up. Some of those who came early felt they had waited long enough and left before the latecomers arrived. Bits of gossip were exchanged as if Fuller was not there, and jokes were made. Occasionally a woman would think to take Fuller's hand, standing to make a little curtsy as she did so. Regina took no part but sat primly next to him, a shy maiden. Her sister only talked to someone invisible in the next house. She seemed to be arguing about the radio.

As they finally settled, Fuller counted thirteen in the six feet by ten room, not including the children. The air was warm and thick with use. A quiet was made for an old lady who delivered into it a long speech in a language Fuller could not identify. Only a small boy being tickled from behind giggled to disturb the gravity. 'What is she saying?' whispered Fuller to Regina, but Regina seemed reluctant to break her silence. The old woman finished and the others gave murmurs of assent.

'What did she say?' Fuller tried again.

'She greeted you.'

'Who is she?'

'She's my relative.'

The tin shack was becoming very hot. Sweat glistened on Regina's bowed neck. Her hands were clasped in her lap; her eyes were on the floor.

'Tell them,' said Fuller, 'that I'm pleased to be here. That I'm happy to meet your relations.'

'You tell them.'

Fuller said it louder. There were approving noises, contending translations. The old woman started on another speech. This time the words were more spirited and achieved a rhythm, the most telling points emphasised with her wrinkled hands and movements of her ear-ringed head. Regina's sister, seeming to be impatient with Regina, began to give an off-hand translation.

'The old lady says she has heard all about you from Regina. All about you! She is happy Regina is with you because she thinks you are a good man. Some white men are not so good but Regina says you are good so they welcome you. She says that when Regina is out at night they would worry but now they do not worry because they know she is with you and that you will look after her. It does not matter that you are loving her without any proper marriage because they know you are like a husband to her.'

Now Fuller could put his finger on it: Regina's demure posture next to him was that of a bride, the perspiration on her neck a sort of blush.

The old woman continued, giving her sentences a ritual seriousness, but the sister waved her hand dismissively and turned away from the room. 'It's just the same things over and over again.'

In the end the woman satisfied herself that her job was done, a conclusion reached, and only music from the tinny radio filled the expectant quiet. After a time Regina hissed, 'Say something.'

'What should I say?' Fuller whispered back, hoping there was a ritual reply to the ritual speech which would satisfy everyone and mean nothing.

'Say what is in your heart,' replied Regina.

He said he was honoured that they thought so well of him,

which was received with approval. He said that he appreciated their trust and hoped he would not disappoint them. This received a mixed response; there was a minor dispute about its meaning. He said he was pleased to have Regina's friendship. This seemed to puzzle them. Fuller sensed that the back of Regina's neck was becoming tenser and that he might humiliate her. More was clearly expected; they were waiting, still willing to give him another chance. Perhaps they wanted to hear that he loved Regina to distraction, wanted to marry her, would always provide for her; perhaps they were even expecting a list of the gifts he would bestow on her – or them. He could not say any of these things and had the feeling that he was trapped in a different dimension from which he could not touch them. He wondered if he had somehow misled Regina. To avoid the silence he said again how pleased he was to meet them all and how he hoped to see more of them in the future. Finally he said that he really ought to return to his hotel soon.

There were loud murmurs, a few people laughed. The old woman looked bad tempered and said in English, 'Go back then. Go back.'

'Shall I give them something?' he asked Regina.

She said nothing. Her sister said, 'Give the old woman something. Five Kangas.' Fuller did. She didn't thank him. 'You can give me your cigarettes,' added the sister.

Outside, where it was cooler, Regina's mood changed abruptly. She smiled and flicked the hem of her dress gaily as if everything had been a great success. 'I'll come to your house,' she assured Fuller. 'I must stay here now.'

37

Dear Sheila,

I woke up in the night with a sudden anxiety about Andrew and Melissa. I hope they are all right. It was two nights ago but they keep coming back into my mind. If you get this letter I would like to know that nothing has happened to them.

I suddenly realised that if anything happened to Melissa or Andrew I would not be able to live with myself. I am not there to look after them and I haven't been for the past five years or so. They seem OK but I feel I should have been there. It can't be all that easy being an adolescent. Easier than it would be here I suppose, but at least here everyone seems to be able to turn to their family. If they lose one bit of it there's always aunts, uncles and cousins. Our children have a very short line of defence.

It's probably too late for me to do anything but suddenly I felt sick that I had neglected the only really important job I had been given – nurturing my children until they are strong enough to stand in the world. I am constantly reminded here how dangerous youth is, how it creates a hope and confidence which is certain to be disappointed. I don't want Andrew and Melissa to be damaged in that way. Perhaps I am worrying unnecessarily – after all they have had a good start in life, a nice home, a good education, a loving mother. Still I might have taught them something if I had been closer. I must know something about the world after all this travel. I don't know what – perhaps only how small we are, how conceited and insignificant are our efforts to give ourselves dignity. Wherever I have gone in the world, power has cared only for itself and not even its possessors have gained dignity from it.

Look Sheila, I'm getting lost again. I would like to write to the children myself, but I don't have the words for it. They would wonder – understandably – why I should suddenly be taking an interest now. They would be right to be sceptical. But if you have received this and you still have some goodwill towards me, will you somehow let them know that I think of them fondly sometimes and that I didn't mean any harm. I still remember them when they were young and they trusted me.

Otherwise, what can I say? The days pass. I sometimes see Jacob but he's really got a lot on his plate these days. He wants me to stay and help him. I see my friend Latif and the girl I told you about – well I'll give her a name: Regina. I say girl deliberately. She's only twenty-two. Baby-snatcher, eh? But twenty-two is not so young here – she had two illegitimate children before she was twenty. Do you mind me telling you this? Latif is not much older. I am beginning to care about these two, for different reasons. Kangaba is such a rough place. Oh well . . .

Give my love to the children. It's time for Andrew's exams isn't it? Wish him luck from me.

Love, Hugh

38

In the Paradise Gardens restaurant Fuller and Regina sat quietly at a table. There was a bottle of beer in front of him, a bottle of Vimto in front of her. A torn piece of paper with a telex message on it was fastened to the centre of the table by the sticky stain left by a soft drink. Occasionally the paper flapped in the breeze from the fan, like a wounded butterfly which wished to leave. Kamara had made an appointment with Fuller and was not yet an hour late.

One of the girls at the Ambassador had brought him the telex message like a trophy. She had always known that Fuller was secretly an important man and now her belief had been vindicated. The telex, she explained, had come to the Sun Hotel where her cousin worked – the government telexes were down these days. Fuller had taken the ragged piece of paper, folded it and put it away in his pocket. 'You don't read it?' she exclaimed, big-eyed.

'I'll read it later.'

'It's a telex! From overseas!' She sounded cheated.

'I'll tell you about it tomorrow. I have to go to the Paradise Gardens.' Fuller smiled easily at her, but he wanted to be seated when he read the message.

Regina was already there when Fuller arrived. She may have been there all day, dreaming of goodness knows what. 'I've a telex from overseas,' he announced and watched Regina's face recording a struggle to comprehend the news and judge its weight.

At last, after Fuller had fetched a beer from the counter, she asked, 'From your English wife?'

'I don't think so. Shall we see?'

Regina pressed her breasts to his arm and furrowed her brow in seriousness. The telex read:

CONSULTANCY TERMINATED EFFECTIVE IMMEDI-

ATELY DUE TERMS OF REFERENCE EXCEEDED STOP
UNDERTAKE NO REPEAT NO FURTHER MISSION AC-
TIVITIES STOP RETURN TO WASHINGTON SOONEST
STOP REGARDS SCHWARTZ

'I can't read this English, Hoo. What does it want to say?'

'It says I have to leave Kangaba immediately because my bosses don't like what I'm doing here.'

Regina stayed silent for a full minute, her proximity to Fuller neither increasing or decreasing, her face hurt and puzzled. Finally she risked appearing foolish to say what was on her mind. 'But Hoo, you don't do anything.'

Fuller nodded. 'You're right Regina. I thought they would complain I was doing nothing. And I thought they wouldn't notice for at least another month – usually they don't very much mind people doing nothing.'

'Are you going home, Hoo?'

Fuller shrugged and turned down his mouth in a frown. The grimace reminded him of trying not to cry as a child and there was something of that in it. 'I don't want to.'

'You can't go home. You belong to Kangaba. Regina will not let you go!'

'I'll have to find out what's going on. It must be the government that has complained to the Bank. It's the only explanation. Perhaps they will deport me.'

They sat back in their tin chairs with no appetite for their drinks. The sheet of telex paper refused to go away. The twilight in the back of the Paradise Gardens felt the safest place to be. The restaurant had found a place for itself just below respectability. Its food – chickenburgers, rice and soup – was eatable and it always had beer after the other places had run out. A girl could – just – go there on her own and not be taken for a prostitute. A man could, just, take a lower-class girlfriend there without her accusing him of being cheap. In the afternoon lull there were only two other customers between them and the door: a man of about fifty in a suit, grubby white cuffs showing, and a very young girl, perhaps thirteen. He leaned close to her and, while she remained petrified with shyness, flashed toothy smiles and swivelled his eyes wildly around the room. Fuller could see, as the girl could not, that the man was equally terrified of losing her and winning her. Beyond them the boy who cooked the chickenburgers dozed by his grill and, beyond him, penniless teenagers danced in and out of the shop entrance, bantering with the half-caste Lebanese behind the counter and carefully calculating the degree to which their poverty allowed them to belong.

'Good,' said Kamara. 'You came.' He slumped down in a chair his legs straight out and pointing at the doorway, then, as if he had tried relaxation and found it useless, he jerked himself upright. There was a bloom of stale sweat on his face and, although no quieter, his voice was hoarser than usual. 'I've just been moving around,' he volunteered. 'I haven't slept for three nights. I don't get tired just moving around.' He turned towards the man behind the counter. 'Bring me soft.' When the Fanta arrived the man waved away Fuller's movement towards his pocket. 'You see,' Kamara observed without looking up, 'the Lebanese want to bribe me now. They want to keep in with me these days.' The half-caste did not react and Kamara's words had seemed automatic.

'I've got trouble, Hugh. I think I should tell you the truth. The police have found some confidential government documents at my house. They are cracking down these days because of all the unrest. I passed some of these documents on to my friends at *Flash* and that's how they found out. Now they want to arrest me. I can't let that happen. I've got to help Kangaba now. Actually, these were some of the documents I collected for you with the letter you and Dr Cesay signed. I have to confess that to you Hugh – I used you to help with our struggle.'

Fuller nodded. 'I suppose I knew. As a matter of fact I'm in trouble too. Now I understand why.' He indicated the telex to Kamara who picked it up and read intently.

'My god, Hugh. What does this mean? Do they want to fire you because of this? That's terrible. I'm sorry. I'm really sorry.'

'It doesn't matter. I don't mind being fired.'

'You don't mind?' Kamara looked up sharply, reassessing Fuller.

'No. But I don't like being chased out of the country.'

'Hoo is a Kangaban,' insisted Regina, briefly deflecting Kamara's look from Fuller.

'Actually, Hugh, I was going to ask for your help. I know I haven't the right, but I wanted to ask you anyway.'

'Go on.'

'You've still got the minister's car and M'bayo?'

'Yes.'

'I have to get out of Kingston and lay low for a while. And there are so many people I have to see around Kangaba. I can only do it in that car.'

'Where are you going?'

'I'll go to my home village. It's far, far away in the north. The government is hardly there. I can base myself there.'

'Can I come?'

'You want to come?'

'I've got to go somewhere.'

'It's OK . . . It's OK. Yes I think it's OK. You can stay in my village. I'll show you Kangaba, Hugh. I want to do that. You're on our side now, I think.'

'I'll just be a passenger.'

'Hoo, Hoo. What about me?' Regina pulled at his shirt sleeve.

Fuller turned to her, then back to Kamara. 'Of course it's a condition that Regina comes with me. The car depends on it. You want to come with me, Regina?'

'I want to. I belong with you. Who is going to cook for you?'

Kamara nodded silently. 'OK. Maybe it's better. We will be less suspicious with a girl in the car. Can you leave tonight, Regina?'

'Tonight?' Fuller was shocked that his decision would be acted on before he had time to reconsider it.

'It has to be tonight. People are being arrested.'
'I'm a Kangaban,' asserted Regina. 'I'm ready to travel.'

They would leave in the evening. Fuller would not return to the Ambassador but Regina would fetch his briefcase. Kamara would disappear and reappear at Regina's house at dusk. Where would Fuller go for the next two hours?

'I'll go to the beach.'
'That's good. They will not look there.'

39

Fuller would remember this, he knew he would. The fish on the beach occurred at intervals, always singly, always dead. They pointed inland with their oversized heads, more skulls than fishheads, and their curved beaks, more birds than fish. They were a foot or two in length, very ugly. He had pointed one out to M'bayo as they parked the car at the edge of the beach. M'bayo had looked disgusted. 'This fish is no good.'

'Don't people eat it?'

'No! People don't eat that!'

To arrive at where they had arrived, the fish, hundreds of them, must have, with a single mind, headed north towards the land and thrown themselves on it to die. It seemed to be their judgement on their own ugliness.

Fuller set out along the beach where a few days before he had walked with Kamara, had received and held Kamara's confession of his doubts. The last palms still reached out across the beach into its clear light, risking their balance and testing their roots, finally shooting up into the sky, a starburst of leaves. The bay still curved, a fine artist's line of white and blue. The waves still reared far out and wavered landward, all elegant glassy edge. Fuller, though, kept his eyes on the sand, fearing the squash of the fat white fish under his sandalled feet, fearing that they might not be dead only lying low, waiting for the opportunity to wriggle further up Kangaba's beach into Kangaba's green, concealing bush.

He would leave with Kamara in the morning – and with Regina. There had been no choice. He walked by the sea, his thoughts not quite smooth – the punctuation of the fish. Behind him, coating the hills, was Kingston, behind that, inland, Kangaba for four hundred miles. It must have been about a month, a month or five weeks. They would be looking for him soon. Schwartz would talk of 'losing his grip', or 'going off the rails'.

Fuller dug at the wet sand with the toe of his sandal, flipped a wedge into the water. He stopped walking and closed his eyes. In Newbury the leaves would be turning soon. Probably there was a railway strike. He opened his eyes and laughed. Let it go, let it go. Ever since his arrival, he now realised, there had been a humming in his ears, the hum of thoughts and words trapped inside him. He closed his eyes again and listened. He heard the surf. His shoulders relaxed and he stretched his arms, shook his hair free. He'd take Regina's love. Why not? He'd trust Kamara's heart. Was there any disturbance he might cause which would not improve Kangaba? 'You're still a young man, Mr Fuller,' came a remembered voice. He laughed again. And Jacob? He couldn't help Jacob. It would be better for Jacob if Fuller disappeared. He turned back, eyeing the fish as he went.

The beach was no longer empty. Near the town three fishing boats were pulled up on the beach, a crowd of women surrounding them. He stopped to watch, discreet against a palm tree. The boats were dugouts with built-up sides and outriggers for sea-going trips. The side boards were brightly painted. An outboard motor was being carried away on the head of a boy, his skull protected by a pad of grass. At first the women bargained noisily mixing aggression and playfulness, then as the light began to fail and the fish had been divided they took up singing and became more serious. The men finished stretching out their nets and slipped away. A group of five or six girls, breasts hardly budding, came forward to join the women, their expressions completely serious. Quickly they were taken into the sea, ducked and, spluttering, were ducked again. As a ceremony it was simple, almost off-hand, but Fuller wondered if he should have been there. He tried to walk on, keeping to the shadow of the palms, anxious again about the prone dead fish. The women saw him, pointed, shouted, made to run towards him. He walked on, wanting to hurry but thinking it foolish and probably unwise. But the women came no closer, instead they stopped to laugh, bending at the waist with mirth. They shouted out lustily, gestured for him to join them. One of the women made a suggestive movement of her hips to the hilarity of the others. The girls, forgotten, stood apart, smiling bashfully. Fuller grinned and waved through the twilight. They were fish-wives after all, he told himself, but still he felt foolish and rueful that, having offered himself to Kangaba, he should have been so immediately put at his unease.

M'bayo, waiting by the Mercedes, had watched all this. 'You must be careful of these fish women,' he told Fuller. 'They like men too much.' M'bayo laughed energetically.

PART III

40

The drive north to Dubeng, a distance of four hundred miles along the main north–south road, lasted two days and a night. Neither Fuller nor Regina knew the way or could calculate the risks and strategies. Kamara, invigorated by nervousness and the sense of movement, gave M'bayo instructions and seemed to want to touch every point in Kangaba. They criss-crossed the main road at intervals but seldom travelled far along it, only joining long enough to register that its quality declined proportional to the distance from the capital. At first the tar was smooth enough for the Mercedes to speed, floating across its pocks and fissures. Further north the pot-holes were sufficiently large to swallow a wheel, forcing M'bayo to dance the car with little swerves, dabs at the brakes and frequent gear changes. Still more remote from Kingston the pot-holes laced together into a treacherous, hopeless surface, beyond skill, far worse than the tracks which had preceded the failed attempt at progress. Here the traffic had made its own road on the footpaths and the bordering fields, only coinciding with the official plan at the single-lane bridges with their skeletons of long crashed vehicles whose drivers had imagined twice the width.

These were only glimpses, small evidences, of the centre's slackening grip. Kamara would say, 'We should avoid that check-point,' and name the town or village, rejecting M'bayo's protests that the ministerial Mercedes would carry them through. Later, Fuller would see from the sun that they travelled for hours west or east, even south, along dirt roads where motor vehicles were rare. Sometimes they were clogged in mud, sometimes racing along footworn tracks, long plumes of dust clouding pedestrians and entire settlements. Once they passed through a wet plain of bright green grass between two forests and Fuller could see in the distance what looked like mangroves and the glint of water. He tried to recall, but could not, the shape of the coastline and how far the inlets reached northwards. Then they were among palm trees, kola-nut trees, rubber trees and great timbers which Fuller could not name and all perspective was lost.

The countryside changed at every turn. Forest gave way to tracts of rice in swamps. For a time the red stalks and deep green leaves of cassava plants were all around and then they were not to be seen at all. In the morning, farms were untidy broadcast crops scattered among the charred stumps of burned out forest hill-sides; in the afternoon, cultivation was tight-packed in tiny fields of high corn and spreading ground-nuts. Then it was forest again and Fuller thought he saw plantations of cocoa, or maybe coffee, before the trees shrank to low, gnarled bush and – for a time – tracts of rocky scrub with scarcely a sign of settlement.

The country belonged to animals as much as man. At the outskirts of villages, goats rushed up to the roadside to stop abruptly, heads high in intelligent consideration, before deciding to dart across or not, the decision sometimes wrong. In the forest south the goats were black and fat, in the north they were brown and spare, built for long savannah treks. Chickens and guinea fowl floundered from the wheels, beating the dust. M'bayo did not slow for them. Yellow dogs raced the car and barked it from their neighbourhoods. A string of monkeys loped across a road with insolent ease, one a mother with her baby clinging to her underside. Baboons sat in judgement on vantage rocks or showed their purple bottoms. A family of wild pigs once charged out of dense forest, trying to make it across the front of the car, its tusked leader running determinedly, seeming to forget, with its big head and powerful shoulders, how puny were the hind legs that propelled it. M'bayo, somehow touched, slowed to let them pass, the last of the line of blindly scampering piglets vanishing victorious into the undergrowth. Among trees the thin legs of deer flickered into invisibility. Sometimes they ran over snakes wriggling urgently over the road's exposed surface and in one place there were dozens, all long and black, all heading in the same direction, which bothered Fuller with their import until he remembered the dead fish on Kingston's beach. The bumps from their hard bodies made him grit his teeth and turn around to watch the spiralling agony of the injured. There were elephants in Kangaba, so Kamara assured Fuller, and lions, but he said that although he, Kamara, could sometimes spot them a foreigner like Fuller never would.

During the first day they stopped a dozen times. At each place Kamara was known, although the villages they visited were a hundred miles apart. Always there were young men in city trousers among the robes and wrappers. There were handshakes and low talk while Fuller, Regina and M'bayo leaned against the car and stretched their legs. M'bayo found ground-nuts, hardboiled eggs and soft drinks, which they consumed as they drove on, the litter turning the car squalid and homely, seemingly invulnerable.

The peoples varied so completely over such short distances that Kangaba came to seem an irreconcilable collection of dislocated parts, the idea of it incomprehensible. For a time they were squat, the men bare-chested with cloths wrapped around their waists, the women bare-breasted. Their settlements consisted of groups of mud huts among the trees, hammocks slung in the shade. Later the villages were much larger with the houses enclosed in fenced compounds, the men wearing flowing robes, the women shy. In a middle-belt of inhospitable rocky savannah, the huts were round and simple, sometimes straw; in other places they were square with tin roofs, collected around noisy, bustling markets.

As the scenery changed so did the languages – but Kamara could always manage. 'I speak five Kangaban languages,' he boasted. 'Not counting English. And a bit of Arabic too. Nobody can tell which tribe I come from. They are mystified. I like that.'

Kamara explained, all the while he explained. He named the tribes, outlined their problems, told Fuller of ancient wars, their relationship to Uncle Funna and the government. He seemed intoxicated by the idea of introducing Fuller to all Kangaba at a single rush, painting Kangaba on to Fuller's blank canvas according to his own design. His words washed over the back seat of the car with the waves of musical warm air which came and retreated through the open windows as M'bayo accelerated and slowed. Fuller gave up questions and discussion – trying to punctuate the wind – to give Kamara his head, letting the sound of his voice be part of the mesmerisation of the journey. Regina dozed against him, jogged, awoke, and quickly slept again, silent and, in her sleep, clinging to him. The sound of the engine rose and fell, and Fuller relinquished, too, all anxiety at M'bayo's driving, seeing only the driver's hand on the gearstick between the front seats, stroking it this way and that, hardly resting. In the middle of the night Fuller woke to find the engine quiet. They were parked within sight of the main road, M'bayo's head resting on the seat-back, mouth wide open, Kamara's eyes closed, his chin on his chest – although he was to deny that he had slept at all. When Fuller next came to, it was still night but the car was moving, Kamara talking low to M'bayo. He slipped away again.

'Hugh, wake up.'

Fuller pulled himself away from dull unpleasant dreams to discover it was day. Regina leaned against him composed in her sleep. He squinted into the sun to see Kamara smiling and holding open the door. Behind him were two girls on a motor cycle. They were skilfully groomed and spotlessly clean. Behind them were low, square government offices on the edge of a town. He pushed himself upright, laying Regina carefully along the seat, and discovered he was very stiff. Kamara was saying something; the girls' faces were animated with confident charm. They seemed improbable. Kamara was saying, 'I want you to meet my friends. They are my sisters somehow.' Two parrots, dazzlingly coloured and raucously loud, flew low over Fuller's head and perched in the tree above the car. The girls giggled as Fuller ducked. He had no idea where they were.

'Good morning, Mr Englishman,' said the girl in front.

'Mr Fuller. His name is Mr Fuller,' corrected the other, and she rested her chin on the shoulder of the first to study Fuller better. Kamara stepped back to watch the girls with Fuller.

'Our motor cycle has no petrol,' confided the first. 'We are without petrol.'

'In fact we have no transport.'

'We have no money.'

'We are immobilised.' They looked at each other, as if delighted.

'We are government community development workers.'

'But our little motor cycle will not take us to any communities.'

'It needs to drink.'

The first girl rocked forward, leaning on the handlebars with her elbows turned inwards so her breasts were pushed forward. Fuller, still half asleep, could not make sense of any of this and his attention became fixed on a thin strand of spittle spanning the perfect teeth and pink gums of the girl. It expanded and contracted with tiny adjustments of her open-mouthed smile. Her friend stroked the girl's unsuitable white blouse with a tender lovingness.

'We have just come to chat.'

'Yes, it's good to chat during time out.'

'Time off. The English say, time off.'

'We only want to loiter.'

'Can we loiter with you?'

Fuller looked to Kamara for help but Kamara seemed to have cast himself as admiring audience to the flirtatious double-act. The girls were young, smart and bore no sign of ever having been touched by anything.

'Niyi has new jeans.'

'Blue jeans.' Niyi obligingly stood up on the foot-rests to show Fuller a smoothly clothed, and shapely, bottom.

'You are friends of Kamara?' Fuller tried to order the world.

'Are we friends of Kamara?' asked one of the other.

'I think we are friends.'

'More sisters.'

'African sisters. We could marry him.'

'Yes we could.'

'But Kamara is never around.'

'No, he's scarce.'

'Sometimes we don't see him for weeks.'

'And then he's here.'

'Your friend Mr Kamara is very mysterious.'

'Sometimes it's months.'

At last, laughing, Kamara rescued Fuller. 'These girls are very strange, they are always together. You would think they had the same mother and father but they do not. They just like to tease the men. Actually, they are my good friends. Can we help them with petrol? Maybe we'll need their help one day.'

Fuller could not imagine how, but he asked M'bayo for the book of government fuel vouchers. 'How much do they need?'

'Not much.'

'Our Honda Seventy just sips.'

'It goes for ever on a little drink.'

'Like a camel.'

'Yes.'

'Not like your Benz.'

'No.'

Kamara passed on the fuel vouchers and told the girls that he had to leave them. Fuller levered Regina upright in her seat and positioned her shoulder against his own. Through the window the two girls smiled and placed little waves next to their smiles. They were immaculate, sexy, incongruous.

'Bye, bye, Mr Fuller.'

'Mr Fuller, bye, bye.'

Near the northern border the main road improved and they rejoined it along with the heavy trucks assembling themselves for the ferry crossing to Upper Guinea. The tail of the long line of trucks waiting outside the border town was already visible when Kamara instructed M'bayo to leave the road for the final time.

'Now we are on my home ground,' announced Kamara. 'We are coming to my ancestral village. Dubeng! Its name is Dubeng. You will see, they claim me even though I am hardly here.'

The track curved between small swamps and then rose into an

area of low forest before dipping again to become a series of little palm-trunk bridges over creeks. At each of these M'bayo slowed, aligned the car, then accelerated across, afterwards smiling back at Fuller with an expression of achievement which made failure at the next seem likely.

A group of women stood in a pond, sinking basket-like nets. 'Mudfish! They are looking for mudfish,' Kamara exclaimed. His commentary became more excited and, Fuller suspected, more unreliable. When they reached the farmland outside the village he claimed to know the proprietor of each tiny irregular plot, giving their names and snatches of their biographies. He told them, absolutely, that the population of the village was five hundred and eighty. Then: 'This is guinea-corn. You call it sorghum.' Fuller thought that the particular crop in question was maize. 'Those are ground-nuts mixed with the cassava.' Fuller felt sure it was beans not ground-nuts. 'These palms are used for palm wine, those for palm kernels and making palm oil . . . Yes, of course we have coconut palms and date palms too. What do you think?' Kamara's national concerns were forgotten in a local pride. 'People come from all over Kangaba – even from other countries – to visit Dubeng because of our koranic school. It is a devout village. No one works on Fridays here.' He had forgotten, too, his disapproval of Islam. 'Look, you see our mosque?' Over the top of a field of ripe millet Fuller could see a shiny tin roof topped by a metal crescent and star. Below it he found the tips of thatched houses.

Closer to the village the track was peopled with villagers return-ing home from a day in the fields or a visit to the border town. They pressed up against corn stalks higher than themselves and Kamara twisted in his seat or put his head out of the window to keep them in view and shout greetings until the looks of puzzled apprehension turned to recognition. Men, women and children in their oldest rags walked with hoes hooked over their shoulders or balanced on their heads. Those who had been to market were smarter, the women in wrappers and blouses tardily pulling a headcloth across their mouths in a formal modesty not shared by the women coming from the fields, whose calves and ankles were thick-caked in mud. 'The women are coming from the swamps,' Kamara explained. 'It's the women who grow the rice here. They feed the family. We depend on the women. They are exploited actually.'

The corn-stalk fences of the first village compounds could hardly be distinguished from the fields which preceded them, but a little further on the village opened up into a pleasant central space shaded by trees – 'Mangoes! Oranges!' – which dappled a floor pressed smooth by feet and picked clean by goats and chickens. Women at the well stared at the car but continued to pull up the bags of water hand over hand. Six or seven elderly men lounged on a platform of branches constructed around the base of a huge irregular tree and, although the appearance of a car must have been exceptional, they did not react more than to return a waved greeting after a long appraising stare.

'You see the platform under the cotton tree? It's the village meeting place – the bantaba. It's our parliament. I'll take you there Hugh. You'll discuss the world with the village elders. I want to hear that.' Kamara's spirits were high. Regina, next to Fuller, said nothing but her grip on Fuller's arm had become tighter and her eyes were unblinking with attention.

'No, no, don't stop yet M'bayo. Let's go. Between those two compounds. The car will go. We have to see the Village Head – the Alkalo. He's my relative somehow. I've even forgotten exactly how. But I'm a member of the founding family – a member of the aristocracy actually. So he must be my relative. OK, stop here. We can walk into the compound, I think.'

Inside the square compound the ground was marked by recent brushing, few footprints spoiling the arcs of someone's whimsical pattern – the sort of pattern that Fuller remembered from the butter of his Nottingham childhood. There were two shade trees and, under their wings, a little group of young citrus, their roots recently watered. Mud-brick buildings cluttered the edges of the compound, some new, some old, records of the households' changing fortunes, the family groups which stayed and those which broke away. 'There are about thirty people living here, the biggest in the village. The Alkalo is the only person to have his own well in his compound.'

Fuller looked around. There were only a few people visible. Two boys returning from the fields stood by the gate behind them, open mouthed, suspended between the twin novelties of Fuller inside and the Mercedes outside. In a far corner, behind a couple of chicken houses on stilts, an oblivious old lady poked a smoky cooking fire. A man – sick, Fuller judged – lay on a grass mat outside the hut, absently fondling a naked toddler. A girl of about twelve dropped her bucket by the well and ran to Kamara in a single movement of eagerness, only to remember herself in time and stop ten feet short to hang her head in murmured formal greeting. Still there was a skip in her step as she acknowledged Kamara's reply and turned to go.

There was an obvious focus in the largest of the houses – the only one to have its walls faced with cement and to have a metal roof, albeit a rusty one. It was set on top of two steps where a group of three women, each with a nursing child, sat plucking ground-nuts from the roots of the harvested plants. 'This is the Alkalo's house. I think it is better that you wait while I tell him you are here.' Kamara spoke to the women who, as one, confirmed that the Alkalo was home. Then he spoke again and made them rock with laughter, looking merrily from Regina to Fuller and back to Regina.

While Kamara was inside Fuller smiled and tried to remember the words for hello but the women's attention was taken by Regina, who stood, still dazed from the journey, in her shiny red party dress and battered high-heeled shoes. One addressed her in Mandinka and Regina became flustered, finding only a couple of stumbled words in reply. Now the women were even more curious and, perhaps thinking it was the question not the language which confused Regina, looked sympathetic and tried a second query which made Regina look to Fuller for help and, not finding any in his face, move closer to him and further from the women whose expressions managed to combine understanding with incomprehension. Fuller, in turn, looked for M'bayo who, like all drivers, spoke a little of everything, but discovered that he had not followed them.

41

The Alkalo was a small man, quite unconscious of his size. He emerged from the doorway ahead of Kamara, paused and briskly hoisted the sleeves of his cotton work robes on to his shoulders before descending the steps with a proper dignity. On his head was an old stained fez, once red, which pressed out a halo of white curls from beneath its rim. He took Fuller's hand between both of his own with a gentle insistency then slipped his grip to bring his right hand to his heart, and Fuller, in the silence, found himself mirroring the easy movement. Kamara laughed. 'He has given you the Moslem greeting. He hopes you are at peace.' Fuller said he was and the Alkalo seemed gratified, turning to Regina and offering her a slight nod of recognition.

Now the Alkalo stood back and, proving his worthiness for headship, extracted himself from the afternoon drowse to make his speech. First he composed himself, placing his cracked feet robustly apart. He ordered Kamara to translate and then he began. The Alkalo wished to welcome Fuller and his wife to Dubeng. He had always liked Englishmen. Even today you would find in his house a picture of the Queen of England alongside that of President Funna. Kamara had explained that Fuller was a good friend who had helped him and this meant that Fuller was also a good friend of Dubeng. Even though Kamara was from the town he was still the son of Dubeng because, unlike townspeople, villagers have long memories. Kamara had told him that Fuller was an important man who had travelled to many places and who was concerned with the problems of people like those in Dubeng. The Alkalo could not imagine these other places but was honoured for Fuller to stay. White people like himself usually only came for a few minutes and left behind them so many mysteries about what they wanted. Fuller would be Dubeng's own white man and would perhaps help them solve these mysteries. It was only right that Fuller and his wife should stay in the Alkalo's own compound and – pointing to a corner near the gate – he had a house for them.

42

The rectangular hut was new, the thatch still yellow, the bricks hardly dry. Inside it was dark, cool and bare – earth floor, earth walls, no windows, a single entrance without a door. The deeper part was half-separated to form a sleeping area. As they crowded in a small animal scampered into the thatch.

Fuller stared into the gloom, the expectant Alkalo standing behind him. The earth smell of an animal's burrow combined with the stale smell of Regina's and Kamara's pressing bodies, unwashed during their journey, and Fuller felt a sudden desperation. He was at Kangaba's northern limit, at the culmination of their two days' motion, staring into a dark earth cul-de-sac. He crumbled; he had gone too far. He was a man who, in Newbury, possessed a four-bedroom bungalow, the sliding doors of which gave out on to a gravel path and the greenest of lawns. By some process which now seemed incomprehensible he was in this black dead-end, a windowless mud hut in a far corner of a country which his Newbury neighbours could not have placed in the correct continent, standing within the smells of poverty and animal existence, about to ingratiate himself to win the charity of a peasant, millions of whom he had bought and sold with the shifting of a decimal point. He took a deep breath as if with the expansion of his chest he would crack the walls, let in the light and expand him to a size which would make midgets of the others. He looked for the way back but could not visualise a destination. Even the first step was elusive. He tried to imagine himself into the hut but could not. Behind him the heat from Regina's and Kamara's bodies seemed to increase and threaten to burn him. For a moment he hated them, but at the same moment he knew he would not turn to them to say, sorry, I've made a mistake, our friendships were a miscalculation, I will return to my own people. He was held stationary and his expansion crumbled dry and useless as mud walls built without straw, leaving

Fuller, even while the others waited for him – all this invisible to them – to rebuild for himself a minimum humanity. It was, he allowed, a suitable reward for presuming to encompass the world, to be offered this, the meanest of homes, in the most obscure of places.

The Alkalo was expectant. Kamara studied Fuller, smiling, watching to see how the old white man would take to living among the poor. Regina pressed closer to him, expressionless.

'Tell the Alkalo it is a fine house,' said Fuller.

'Is a bush house!' Regina whispered fiercely into Fuller's ear, the stern judgement of a town girl.

When the Alkalo had left, Kamara slapped Fuller on the back, his spirits still high. 'Don't worry, Hugh, soon things will change in Kangaba. You will not have to live here for ever. We will need some old men like you to help us after liberation. We will need old heads to balance our young ones. I want you for my adviser.' He had not been so reckless before or stated his ambitions so boldly.

M'bayo joined them as they returned to the car for their bags. 'This is a good village,' he announced. 'We don't have such land in my part of the country. I will grow onions!'

'You're looking happy,' observed Kamara. 'Have you found a place to stay?'

'Yes I've found a good place!'

Kamara turned to Fuller. 'You see these drivers? He is only in the village for an hour and he has already found a woman.'

'No!' M'bayo protested, but his old face looked bashful and the exhaustion of the journey had been washed from it.

'Anyway,' Kamara continued to Fuller, 'it should be good for you too. You will discover what it is like to be a peasant. One of your banks even had a project here. You are supposed to look at projects, isn't it? That's your job.' He laughed and dared to slap Fuller's back a second time.

'We need a Vono bed,' declared Regina in a sort of acceptance.

43

On his first night in Dubeng Fuller could not sleep. Their bed was a frame of bamboo and twine with a straw mattress. He imagined all sorts of life inside it, biting him and passing on African diseases against which he had no defence. 'Tomorrow we will buy a Vono bed,' said Regina, half asking, half stating. Fuller nodded in the dark and turned again to try and sleep. He remembered the chicken-house built on stilts to protect it from the snakes and wondered what protected them. The animal in the thatch – a lizard, a mouse, a rat – was active in the night and once lost its grip to fall with a flat slap on the hard ground before clambering back up the wall. Perhaps the next time it would land in their bed and wriggle between them. The mosquitos circled in, only falling silent when they were ready to bite.

The day started early with a cock that crowed before dawn. Fuller was relieved to give up the fight for sleep but was unready for the day. There was no coffee in Dubeng but Oumie, the Head's senior wife, brought sweet tea and took Regina away to show her the well and the kitchen hut. Fuller, red-eyed, sat on a grass mat, leaned against his briefcase and wondered morbidly how he would spend his time.

The border town eight miles from Dubeng used all the high ground among the riverain swamps and clearly needed more. It was no place for a town but the river and the border had combined together to make it the place where man was twice delayed – once by nature, once by history. Two ancient chain ferries – one always out of action – crossed the river between Kangaba and Upper Guinea and were never enough for the traffic. To this was added a confusion of customs, immigration, tax collection and vehicle weighbridge formalities on both sides. The traffic laid siege to the river but neither the angry crowds nor the heavy reinforcements of trucks backed-up a mile down the road could make it yield; it continued, wide, placid and aloof, catching, for a time, the flat-decked ferries and the towering trucks within its calm.

The town catered to the needs of the twice-delayed. There was a cluttered market-place with open sewers which did not drain and around it bars and the sort of cheap hotel which did not provide sheets. Smuggling made it the best market in Kangaba. Transistor radios, cassette-players and fertiliser came from Upper Guinea in exchange for kola-nuts and illegal charcoal. Kamara led Regina and Fuller past all this without explanation, ignoring the restaurants with their open fires, the rows of curtained cubicles for cheap prostitutes, and the stalls selling patent medicines for ills made worse by the swamps, until they reached an alley of black-market money-changers, where Fuller discovered he was eight times richer than he had imagined.

They shopped. Fuller, tired and disorientated, let Kamara bargain and Regina choose, letting them take money from his hand as they needed it. They bought: a metal bed frame, lacquered black with appliquéd pink flowers, a matching mattress, a set of colourful enamel cooking pots, mats for the floor, cloth for a door curtain, tinned food, a cassette-player with spare batteries and a vacuum flask made in China. 'Come on, Hugh,' Kamara insisted. 'You are the husband. You have to choose.' But Fuller hung back, hoping for invisibility, while Regina seemed to possess a fully imagined idea of what was right for them in their new life in Dubeng.

The border town drew Fuller. On the second day he took the Mercedes and visited it on his own, and again on the third, fourth and sixth days.

He was uneasy in the village, unable to talk and unable to hide from the curious stares. There was no place for him and its intimacy disturbed him, preventing his mind from running free. In spite of his insisting that the water should be boiled, he had diarrhoea, which left him too weak to rise to Kamara's invitations into village conversation. He felt that nature had taken and hidden him in this rural place and would now decompose him at its will. Regina looked at him and went about her work – he imagined her dismayed at his helplessness. His mind turned to aeroplanes but, instead, he took the car keys from M'bayo and drove the eight miles into town as if he were visiting a city and found an open-fronted tea stall where he drank in the shadows, as if it were a Paris café.

For hours Fuller would watch the chaos at the ferry while the Moslem stall-holder poured and repoured tea from a tall Arab teapot, measuring his skill by the height of the fall, starting close and extending his arm high while the glass filled, then drawing pot and glass together as smoothly as a concertina, not spilling a drop even as it brimmed. Fuller did not know whether the ritual was to brew the tea or cool it but he found the rhythm soothed him. The stall-holder ignored him, leaving him to lean back in the only chair, resting up against the stock – sacks of grain, boxes of tinned sardines and Blue Band margarine.

There was more to gaining the ferry than waiting. Official business had priority, rich officials absolute priority. They jumped the queue in spurts of acceleration while the cheated and the democratically-minded pounded on their roofs and tried to block their way. A VIP whose car injured a boy was pulled to the ground together with his driver and only the action of armed police saved their lives. Below the absolute rights of rank and wealth, other contenders argued for their particular advantage – a cousin who went to school with the man who directed the vehicles on to the ferries, a brother in a high position. Money and documents proving some connection somewhere were waved in gesticulating hands, voices were raised, people pushed. Fuller saw from his seat in the shadows that a man without money, connections, charm, persistence, spirit, had no chance at the border; he would stay on the wrong side forever.

*

As Fuller was leaving for his fourth and final visit to the tea shop – the villagers sad and puzzled at his departures – Kamara ran to him. 'Hugh, I'm coming with you. I want to catch a lorry at the border town.'

'Actually,' Kamara explained as they drove to the town, 'I have stayed too long. I know I am missed these days.'

It had not occurred to Fuller that Kamara might not stay with him, although, of course, it was obvious. He put aside feelings of panic and annoyance before offering at the lorry park: 'Safe journey, Latif. We'll be waiting for you.'

He had assumed the Mercedes would not be noticed in the bustle of the ferry traffic or, if it was, it would be ignored under a general immunity from law and morality, but on this final visit to the tea shop Fuller saw a solitary young SDF gunman approach the car, big eyes fixed on the mud-caked number plate. More of a boy than a man, the gun on his back was a real burden. He bent towards the plate then drew back, demanding something of the tea shop proprietor in a voice which lacked command or conviction. The proprietor showed no respect, did not look up, offered only a single word in reply, spat. Now the SDF boy seemed dissatisfied and Fuller watched intently – imagining a raised alarm and people running – as he leaned towards the plate a second time and touched the mud with graceful two-tone fingers, brushing it lightly. Already Fuller missed Kamara with his confident explanations and sureness about the way things worked in Kangaba. The boy halted in his movement, reconsidered, choosing then to wipe his fingers on his trousers. Fuller felt suddenly confident of knowing the boy's mind and he willed it on its course: Mercedes cars belong to powerful men; the outcome of initiative cannot be calculated; there is only the certainty that the less powerful will lose. Decisive at last, the boy slipped away towards the crowd of cars and trucks disputing their turn at the ferry and made gestures at them to move in the ways they were already moving.

When Fuller left the border town an hour later, passing the line of battered trucks and their sleeping drivers, he felt relieved to be going home.

44

The women of the compound, the Alkalo's wives and the wives of his sons – bolder than the men, bolder than Regina – took Fuller in hand. While Regina looked on, wondering that Hoo could be treated so, the women tried him out at village work. First they had him picking ground-nuts from the harvested roots, marvelling at his slowness, him using both clumsy hands while they managed with one, the other holding a nursing infant to their breasts. They made him sit with them on a mat and when he couldn't get comfortable – and their husbands were not in sight – they tried to bend him forcibly to sit as they sat, back straight, legs splayed flat on the ground. They had never met a human so inflexible. When Fuller finally rolled over on his back with his legs in the air, plants scattered, all work stopped for general laughter, bringing the Alkalo from his house to scold – but not subdue – his womenfolk.

Next they wanted him to hoe. White men had sometimes come to Dubeng to talk to them about farming but, they said, they had never seen a white man hoe. Fuller made signs to say that he too had never used an African hoe and, when they were incredulous, Regina confirmed it to them in her halting Mandinka. Never hoed! Was there such a person? Oumie, a woman made patient by life, demonstrated, holding the hoe with both hands, biting the ground with it and shuffling backwards between strokes, an efficient, rhythmic movement producing a line of broken ground. Fuller tried to copy her but his knees were bent, the hoe struck unevenly and his movement was full of clumsy effort. It was true, they agreed, he had never hoed in his life.

By the time the rest of the household was arriving back from the fields the wish to try Fuller out on every task and rediscover the extent of their own abilities had gained a firm hold. The men formed an outer fringe to the audience, caught between fascinated amusement and disapproval of a man doing women's work.

Fuller proved perfectly competent at drawing water from the well and impressed them with his strength in operating the ground-nut sheller. No one seriously thought he would have any success at catching chickens and he didn't. The most outrageous experiment came later when two girls took out their poles to pound the rice. Indisputably it was a job for young women and they worked bare-breasted, one bringing her pole down hard while the other stood back and threw hers clear. The girls found their rhythm and under the eyes of Fuller and their elders gave themselves to the work, their bodies soon shiny with perspiration, lovely and vibrating with the movement. The men, who had been hanging back, pressed closer to Fuller and the women.

Oumie stopped the girls who, deprived of movement, stood awkward and proud in front of the audience, catching their breath. She took a pole from one of the girls and gestured to Fuller. Everybody laughed. Fuller moved towards the wooden pounding bowl but was stopped by Regina – now lively and entering into the spirit of it all – who insisted, to general approval, that Fuller remove his shirt.

He stood in front of the girl who was to be his partner watching her closely. She brought her pole down. Fuller brought his down and lifted it, she brought hers down again and Fuller followed, but was too slow in lifting clear so her next descent tangled with his. Oumie gave more tuition. He must not just lift it but throw it high – so! Follow the girl. Fuller prepared himself – it was becoming dark and the audience intent. The girl dropped her pole, Fuller his. She increased the pace, he kept up. He was sweating, mesmerised by the rhythm, entranced by the shiver of the girl's breasts when her pole made impact and finally, it took the touch of Oumie's hand drawing him back to extract him from this world. There was applause. Oumie said he was dangerous, this man, he looked at the girl's breasts instead of the pole. His lustfulness would be the death of him if he didn't move his head away more quickly.

As reward one of the men dipped a plastic cup into a bucket

of palm wine and handed it to Fuller. He looked down into it and saw the tiny translucent maggots dancing there. He was thirsty, this was Dubeng: he drank the wine.

45

The night after his rice-pounding demonstration Fuller slept through the sound of the cock's crow and through Regina's rising. When he woke from his dead sleep to a compound already settled to its daytime quiet, he discovered that his stomach, undergoing a parallel adjustment to his mind, had settled and hungered for the bulk of rough-grained rice splashed with peppery soup. A new health was eager to prove its superiority to illness and demanded that it be used and the time wasted by its perverse relative reclaimed. He wound a cloth around his waist and pulled aside the entrance curtain. The sun was high. Those who were going to the fields had gone. Regina sat across the compound on the steps of the Alkalo's house, sewing with a couple of the younger wives and their infants. An old man dozed under a shade tree, one thin leg bent up into his armpit, a string of prayer beads resting in his open palm. The women, the previous night still alive for them, called a greeting; Fuller smiled back and flexed his muscles in mock triumph. While her companions laughed, Regina smiled her cautious smile until it reached its fullest glow, then kept it there as if photographing Fuller standing in the doorway dressed in his wrapper, looking happy. She left her friends and came to him, stopping short in the village way, not looking him in the eye, in the village way, but, out of sight of the others, peeping up at him to share this joke of their new way of things.

He could not live like this. No! It was not the time for eating but Regina had found him rice and sat opposite him while he ate, sprinkling a little of the sauce over the rice nearest to him before he took it in his fingers, tossing a scrap of fish to his side of the plate, feeding her man with delicacies. No, declared Fuller, it was time they fixed up the house, wasn't it? They had the money and he had seen all sorts of things in the market at the border town. Regina glowed but did not speak. She took a piece of chicken meat, red and shiny with pepper and palm oil, and pressed it slowly into Fuller's mouth, interrupting his talk for a few moments. 'We don't have to live exactly like the others. We can make our house comfortable. After all we are from Kingston. Do you think it would cause trouble if we lived better than the others?'

'What trouble, Hoo?'

'I mean would it make them feel jealous? Would it make me seem more important than the Alkalo?'

Regina laughed, then was serious. 'No, Hoo, it would not be troublesome. They would be happy. They think it strange that we live like them. I think you are disappointing them. So far they have only seen the car. They keep asking me if you are poor. They want to learn from you.'

'What do you want then, Regina?'

'Is up to you, Hoo.'

Fuller said, well, he had seen a two-ring gas stove in the market and there was French bottled gas smuggled over from Upper Guinea. It would save cooking over a wood fire. Would Regina want one of them?

'Is a good idea, Hoo.'

And there were paraffin lamps, which were much better than candles. And now he thought of it, he really didn't feel comfortable sitting eating on the ground. If he bought some wood in town and some nails, he could make a table and chairs – or at least a bench. A water filter would be a good thing too. Perhaps he could even find some way of rigging up a shower using an oil drum . . .

'Maybe,' ventured Regina as Fuller's vision faltered, 'some cups and saucers.'

'Yes, of course. And we need a tin-opener.'

'We need something to make it more comfortable. Some carpet. Cushions. Pictures!'

'Don't forget the refrigerator . . . and a washing machine. And a fireplace. English houses have fireplaces. You are an English wife now.' He spilt rice with his hand as he gesticulated expansively.

Regina, pushing the spilled rice into little piles, protested over his laughter, her voice piping high. 'No, no, Hoo. Is not true. I'm not an English wife. You are a Kangaban husband.' Then grabbing back at something which should not be forgotten she added, 'You can get refrigerators. I've seen bush refrigerators. They use paraffin.'

'No,' replied Fuller firmly, 'I draw the line at refrigerators. I mustn't spoil my bush wife.'

Fuller decided they should have windows and, although the Alkalo warned him that they would make the house hotter and let the insects in, he hired a group of young men to knock two holes in the wall. The Alkalo was right, but Regina did her best with curtains.

The group of young men – boys, really, in their mid-teens – became regular visitors. They explained that at their age they had to work on their fathers' farms and had no money of their own. It was customary for them to offer the community their labour as a group so they could save money together. 'What do you want money for?' Fuller asked. Their spokesman, Mustapha, who had been to school, replied, 'Young men's things. Celebrations, money to get married, cassettes.' 'Palm wine,' added Regina, making them bashful.

Fuller invented work for them. His home would have its own latrine – a deep pit was required with a guinea-corn fence round it. Why not a porch? It was not in the village style but, under Fuller's direction, they extended the roof thatch forward and supported it on rough-hewn branches. The shower was the most ambitious project and was never completely successful, but when finished it was possible to climb up and pour water into the oil drum and then quickly run underneath while the water drained lazily through holes punched in the bottom.

The rest of the village was intrigued by the flurry of ingenuity. When, out of hearing of their fellow villagers, they came to Fuller to ask who was to have the table when he left, or could they be first in line to make an offer on the cooker, Fuller's reply was always, 'Who said we are going to leave?' leaving the questioners embarrassed and bemused.

Regina explained to Fuller that some of the chickens which wandered in and out of their door did, in fact, belong to them. 'It's foolish not to have chickens,' she said firmly. 'They don't cost anything.' The two girls, about twelve years old, also appeared at this time. They helped Regina prepare food and clean the house and, although they were respectful of Fuller, it was clear to him that they felt answerable only to her. As far as Fuller could establish they were from poor families and, in return for food, they were to help Regina with the household chores. Their assignment as her apprentices was a tribute to Regina's worth in the eyes of the village – and to Fuller's money.

One morning, watching the girls raise dust as they brushed the earth floor, Regina said, 'Hoo, this bush floor is no good. Too much dust. We should have a cement floor.'

'Isn't that a big job?'

'No, it's a small job. They have cement in town.'

It was all done in a morning. Mustapha's work group made a thin cement and spread it straight on to the dirt. When they finished the floor they started, under Regina's direction, on the walls, coating the mud inside and out to turn everything grey.

A few days later, returning from a walk down to the river to help M'bayo plant his onions on the irrigated land, Fuller was stopped short at the entrance to the compound. While he had been away the boys had limed the outside walls of the house white and, caught unawares, Fuller saw nothing less than a thatched Devonshire cottage. He laughed out loud. Regina, alarmed, came to him and asked why he was laughing, didn't he like their white house? 'I don't know,' replied Fuller, 'I just never imagined anything could be so simple.'

46

Fuller's days gained rhythm, which, in the way that drumming makes farm work go faster, took away his sense of time. Fridays, the day work stopped and the other men wore their best clothes, caught him by surprise. There was little more that could be done to the house and little reason to make further visits to the market in the town. A piece of the compound fence was removed and the Mercedes was pushed inside where, as if it were an established custom – though it must have been unprecedented – the children set about covering it with a thatch of palm fronds. They found, perhaps, something jarring in the hardness and shininess of the car's metal.

Several days a week Fuller worked on the Alkalo's farms, either helping with the harvest or preparing the land near the river where irrigated vegetables were grown during the dry season. He was inept and at first the Alkalo was shocked by his offer of help. Fuller explained that he needed the exercise, which was met first with incredulity and then with laughter. Only when he explained it in traditional terms would the Alkalo agree. It was true, wasn't it, that there was a custom of 'strange farmers' coming from other places, even other countries, to farm in Dubeng for a year? This was true. And wasn't it the custom that in return for housing and a plot of land they would also work on their host's land? Yes, this was also true . . . but Mr Fuller was English, he was not a young man saving for marriage, he had not come at the beginning of the farming year. 'Never mind,' replied Fuller, 'I want to work on your farms like any other strange farmer.' The Alkalo considered, decided finally on delight, and warmly took Fuller's hand in both of his.

It was past the busiest time of the farming year and Fuller made his own habits. Usually he would walk to the fields with one of the Alkalo's married sons – the Alkalo himself, though no older than Fuller, had retired from physical work – soon after daybreak, a hoe hooked over his shoulder. At this time of day the air still had some cool in it and, from the upland fields, the low sun played dazzling games with distant curves in the river. When he tired, he sat under the makeshift shelters of the young boys who kept the birds off the ripening grain and he finally mastered the yard-long sling shots they swung around their heads – though his stones rarely went near the birds. It was here among the unselfconscious children who had learned a little English in school, that Fuller risked his first sentences of Mandinka.

In the afternoons he rested with Regina on their Vono mattress, on their Vono bed. They made love. Regina, along with her dresses and heels, had shed her busy skills and lovemaking became a habitual, almost unconscious thing. They discovered that lying on top of each other was all too hot, too energetic. Instead, Regina's bottom daily found its way into Fuller's lap as he lay curled beside her and, touching only at that point, they slumbered through the afternoon, Fuller awakening from a shallow, timeless sleep to find himself erect and inside her, she moving, emerging next into consciousness to find himself spent and outside. His spine these days seemed made of a different substance, cooler and more flexible. He had reached an agreement with the insects too. And the lizards.

The girls who helped in the house started school in the border town. Fuller paid for the fees and uniforms. They walked the eight miles there and the eight miles back, exercise books held over their heads to protect them from sun. Their arrival back in the house in the afternoon told Fuller and Regina that it was time to get up from their siesta. Hot and tired from their walk the girls had taken up the habit of drinking water from the water filter in the living room as soon as they returned. When Fuller stumbled up from bed, from Regina, a cotton wrapper tucked around him, the girls would be undressing, gratefully freeing themselves of the perspiration-marked white blouses required by school regulations. Fuller, still warm and sleepy, treasured their welcome and their musky presence, and did not misunderstand it.

47

Kamara returned after three weeks. Fuller saw him standing at the compound gate and went to greet him.

'Latif, welcome home. Are you all right?'

Kamara stood staring at the house and then, ignoring Fuller, started walking towards it. 'My goodness,' he muttered. 'My goodness, I was not expecting this . . . Yes, I'm all right. No problem . . . You've made yourself a palace.' He shook one of the branches supporting the porch to test its strength, did the same with the rickety bench. 'Is this the same hut I remember from before I left? What's this? A gas cooker?' He turned to Fuller and gave him a warm, amused look of appraisal. 'And you look well, Hugh. You are losing your white man's softness. I think you have become a peasant.' He picked up the cassette player. 'A rich peasant.'

Kamara talked about his trip but avoided the detail of his own role in things, which was nevertheless defined by the shape of what he described. Fuller did not press. The situation in Kingston had not improved. A little rice was available on the black market but government officials and the Syrians were hoarding in expectation of a rise in the official price. He had heard that the IMF wanted it too. There had been a demonstration outside the Treasury in Kingston by the junior government employees, who had not been paid for two months. At the end of the month, instead of money or cheques, they received a stencilled piece of paper which explained that, as loyal citizens, they had volunteered to give their salaries to the National Revival Fund. The demonstration had been broken up by the SDF and nine people had been shot. Since then everyone with any sort of criticism of the government had been arrested or had run away. None of the dockworkers who Fuller had met in the literacy class were to be found. The friends of Kamara who were not arrested had gone to the bush to join up with other friends. 'It's a tinder box,' Kamara declared and, further exercising his command of English idiom, added, 'It is a powder keg . . . I fear for the future, I really fear. If they announce a price rise or do not release rice soon, everything will just explode. I have never seen my aunt helpless before. All the conditions for revolution are there now, actually. We have to move quickly now.'

Fuller held back from questions and reminded himself that the situation was real even if the theory was suspect and that his knowledge was not superior to Kamara's. When, at last, Kamara broke the silence it was to return to the sort of conversation he seemed to enjoy as recreation, its content oddly divorced from Kangaba. 'What about Lenin, Hugh? What do you think about Lenin? I think he was the real hero.'

It seemed to Fuller, as he sat with Kamara on the bench under the porch, that at some point during Kamara's three-week absence, they had become friends. A balance of weights had been established which left them both easier in each other's company than with the villagers. In spite of Kamara's family connection with Dubeng, Fuller understood that he was more of the town than the village. The men at the bantaba listened to Kamara's ideas, but they remained foreign ideas, always less digestible than a novel teaching from a fashionable Moslem marabout. It was to Fuller he gave his confidence and confessed his fears.

Kamara had three disciples in Dubeng. These young men followed him around and sometimes came to Fuller's house to sit on Fuller's bench. Often they helped themselves to Fuller's palm wine, but not so much that they would not be invited back. Unlike most men in the village they wore torn trousers and flapping shirts instead of robes and among themselves they often talked in a defiant pidgin English. They could not knuckle down to a lifetime of repetitive farm work for tiny reward and they were the despair of their families.

The story of the three young men was that they had left the village some five years before, at the time of 'the project', in order to seek work in Kingston. Each had held out as long as he could: until his distant relatives would no longer feed him; until the last friend of a friend who might introduce him to a job had become impatient; until, as they told it, they were tired of being hungry or, as some said, the police and the victims of their thefts were hot on their heels. Returning penniless had been a humiliation and they clung to their claims of city sophistication with a useless pride. They said they were angry with the rich, corrupt men in Kingston whose wealth was impossible to touch and they were angry at their fathers and that Moslem talk about rewards going to those who led good Moslem lives. Kamara's confident analysis of what was wrong with Kangaba and his explanations at the bantaba that what had happened to them was not their fault, soothed their damaged pride, the sound of his confident voice more important than the detail.

On evenings when Kamara was in Dubeng the three town boys sometimes stayed on Fuller's porch to play cards or a local variant of draughts – larger and more complex than the version Fuller had played with his mother in Nottingham. They liked to carry Fuller's table outside – there were only two tables in Dubeng, his and the Alkalo's – and show the other villagers how things were done in Kingston. They told Fuller, hoping for disapproval, that they liked to gamble, but none of them could practise this heresy since they rarely had a coin between them.

48

The bantaba was a place which Fuller came to love. There was a time between dusk and sleep when the village caught its breath; the noises of the day were dying and the animal noises of the night had yet to gain strength. Only the donkeys, forever oblivious to their surroundings, might break the quiet with their heart-wrenching hoarse barks, a call of distress which had no cause or remedy. At this time, it seemed to Fuller, the true spiritual life of the village – not that of the mosque – was renewed. Men joined the bantaba with the quietest of greetings and drifted from it without explanation. Those who stayed found themselves comfortable spots among the weave of logs and branches which made up the platform. Those with tobacco, smoked. Others, like Fuller, merely dreamed, communing with the countless stars visible through the branches of the cotton tree. The night sky seemed a gentle hand placed on them.

Sometimes there was talk, usually desultory. Often no one would make the effort. Only when Kamara was in the village would the mood change. He would join them and provoke the older village men into talk. Fuller admired his energy: to care so much. The men were good-natured about it, fond of Kamara and secretly excited by the chance to present their lives as events of a larger significance. Kamara's three disciples, too junior for the bantaba, sat on the fringes and nodded gravely, offering single words of accord too quiet to be challenged.

Kamara was skilful at talking with the village men. He kept a lively spark in his eyes and maintained a mischievous and affectionate smile. Much was forgiven him. He prodded the old men's dreaming minds until it seemed to one or the other that the effort to argue or reminisce was worthwhile. He made them tell stories of forty years before when the village had, they said, more food and a greater variety of it. In those days – oh yes, they all agreed, eyes large with memory – they would make a feast for any visitor and the grain stores were always full. If Fuller had come to Dubeng in those days there would have been such a celebration – they would have killed a goat, there would have been fish from the river, eggplant, peppers, okra, bitter tomatoes, pumpkin and vegetables which they did not even see any more these days. And palm wine. Of course, they added with a sidelong look at the koranic teacher, they were less enlightened about the undesirability of alcohol in those days.

Kamara led them on. What did they think had changed? Oh, it was not so easy to say. The rains, of course, were not what they had once been. Perhaps they had not been as good Moslems as they should. And on the upland there was no longer empty land between the villages. Where they had once left ten years between cultivations they now sowed every year. That was part of it too. Then the young people did not like work and were tempted by the sinful towns. And the new seeds and chemicals were not as good as the old farming methods. While Kamara waited and listened to these old men's explanations his disciples whispered 'imperialism' and 'exploitation', confidently anticipating him, and the old men would become rattled by the strange new version of the world these words suggested – at which point Kamara rescued them. No, he rebuked the dissenters, the old men were right, it was just as they said, these were indeed the ways in which life had become hard. When they talked about the new farming methods and the lack of land, they were really complaining about the way the introduction of cotton and ground-nut cash crops by the British had undermined the food supply. You see, this is the way that exploitation works. Now everyone had to pay taxes and everyone was in debt for farm inputs so you had to sell more cash crops and food to the government. Is that not so? Gratefully, the old men agreed it was exactly what they had meant. And, Kamara continued, nobody could earn a decent living in the village any more, so of course the young people would rather go to the town – it was all connected. This time it was the young men who said he had got it exactly right: there was nothing in the village. Yes, and the government controls the crop prices, doesn't it, so you have to work harder each year just to earn the same amount. Ask Mr Fuller, Kamara instructed them, he knows why this is. You are lucky to have him here, don't waste him. Ask him whether you get a fair price for your ground-nuts.

Fuller was drawn in, a witness from the other side. He agreed that it was true that farmers only received a fraction of the world price for their crops. Also he could not contradict Kamara when he said that much of the difference went to pay interest on loans from foreign banks. The villagers looked at Fuller, trusting him, but finding it difficult to join together the pieces of a jigsaw which made a picture far larger than the world they saw. Kamara would then stay quiet, watching the burning of the fire he had kindled in the old men's minds.

On these nights, to the confusion of their wives, the men returned to their homes excited and still talking. Regina reported to Fuller that the womenfolk were alarmed on these nights and feared an upsurge of reckless enthusiasm among the men, the sort of foolishness of which only men are capable. But the excitement never outlived the duration of Kamara's visits, which lasted ten days, then six days, then two. Left to themselves, the evenings on the bantaba became peaceful again, filled with resting muscles, curling smoke and the countless stars – perhaps a distant clink of pots from where the women worked on, which was as it should be.

Three old men, one of them the koranic teacher, questioned Fuller in Kamara's absence, a confusing transaction combining Mustapha's slight English with Fuller's few words of Mandinka. First they asked whether he agreed with everything Kamara said, to which Fuller replied that he thought Kamara had a good heart but he could not agree with everything. Certainly Kamara was very clever, but he was, after all, still young. Fuller's circumspect visitors liked this reply to their question and, encouraged, asked another: what god did Fuller believe in? Was it the white man's god? At first Fuller tried to explain, wanting to be honest, that he belonged to no religion and probably could only conceive of god as the higher part of man, but no fraction of this seemed to survive Mustapha's translation. Seeing the growing confusion, and fearing it would develop into annoyance, Fuller stopped Mustapha in his efforts. 'Tell them I'm a Christian,' he amended. Relief and understanding replaced the confusion and Mustapha seemed pleased to have done his job. 'They say this is what they thought. They say Jesus was a prophet for Allah so it is all right. You have the same god.' Fuller agreed and, this communality established, there were smiles and handshakes. The koranic teacher, in particular, was gratified – it was just as he had told the villagers it would be – and told Fuller that when Kamara returned to translate he would tell him the history of Dubeng. Fuller said he would look forward to that.

49

Regina discovered that the village women respected her. She held the novelty of respect to her as if it were a lover she expected soon to lose. Fuller noticed a new reserve, the adoption of a queenly bearing. Her walk from the well, an earthenware pot on her head, was slower and more stately than the other women. She replaced her dresses with wrappers and tops of printed cotton, keeping her breasts covered with the dignity of an older woman. Instead of her scraped spiky heels she wore rubber flip-flops.

The other women watched Regina, fascinated that a woman of the city, who spoke English, whose man was a white man, could act as they acted and be as they were. To Fuller's admiration her market-place Mandinka quickly blossomed into a means of communication with which she could sit with the Alkalo's wives and talk about this and that, her hands, like those of her companions, leaving the work in her lap to gesticulate in emphasis or scandalised disgust. They came, while Fuller was away, to Fuller's house to admire the bottled-gas cooker, and in return taught Regina how to make bean cakes, soap and tie-dye cloth. Sometimes, in bed, Regina turned to Fuller wordlessly and hugged him with all her strength so that he knew he had, by accident, given her something too important to be named.

In their fourth week in Dubeng Regina received conclusive proof of her acceptance by the village women. A group of a dozen women, all mothers and respected, came to their house one evening. Fuller was sitting outside on the bench, his back pressed against the wall. It was Regina they wanted to see; they were a delegation. Humbly, Fuller went inside to tend the rice while Regina carefully re-fastened her wrapper, smoothed her blouse and slipped her feet into her sandals before going to welcome the visitors. She greeted each of them by precedence and name and distributed calm while the seating on mats and stones and stools was scrupulously negotiated, the more junior women deferring to the more senior in choice of seat and position. Fuller saw that Regina had expected this, the meeting was not a surprise. She insisted that the senior women, the oldest wives of the Alkalo, the koranic teacher, the wealthier farmers, should sit above her on the bench – after all she was younger and, as they all knew, her knowledge of important skills was slight and generally she was only of the level of a junior wife, hardly more than a silly girl. But, no, the women were of a single mind, Regina was a woman of a superior kind, knowledgeable in city ways which were to them only the source of fear and mystery. She could write, she could speak English, they had come to ask for help.

As Regina knew, they, the women of Dubeng, were very poor. But, as she also knew, they worked hard and besides growing the rice to feed their families they were famous throughout the region as producers of vegetables and makers of fashionable blouses. In the past they had tried to help themselves but it had come to nothing. When they took produce to town the traders cheated them in so many ways because the village women did not understand town cunning and could not understand the sums they used to calculate their money. If they went to the government cooperative it was worse. There they weighed the produce while the women only knew how to measure by volume – which everyone could see was fair – and then they cheated them by only giving a piece of paper – a 'receep' – which they could never turn into money. The government always used paper and writing which were mysteries to them. Of course they had asked their men to help, but Regina knew what men were like, they just made a lot of noise and promises which came to nothing, leaving the women with the work as usual.

No, we women, they concluded from innumerable experiences of disappointment, must help ourselves. Never mind the men. Look, we have saved this. In a measured gesture of absolute trust Oumie handed to Regina an enamel pot heavy with coins.

They explained that the women met every week and each contributed the same amount to the pot. It used to be that each woman would in turn take the weekly total for her own use but they found that such little amounts were only little help. If they wanted to do something useful they needed to accumulate their money over a long time, which they had done. But now they were scared to use it. When they had first loaned some money from the savings to one of the group for her child's school fees there was an argument over the amount and, because they could not write, there was no record to settle the dispute. But they respected Regina and she could write – they had seen her write messages for Mr Hoo. And she had lived in Kingston among all sorts of people. The small government people in the border town, so far from the capital, would certainly listen to a woman like Regina with a husband like Mr Hoo.

Regina waited, hands in lap, until each woman had said her piece, the presentation was complete. Then she said, her voice deliberately small, that she was honoured by their request and, although she feared they overestimated her abilities, she would be pleased to do her best. She thought they should count the money and discuss among themselves what might be bought with it – didn't they agree?

At bedtime, when Fuller wanted to sleep, Regina lay awake, her mind excited. What did Hoo think? If they bought a treadle sewing machine – a 'Singer' – would the women be able to sell the extra blouses that they made? And were the women wise in wanting to buy fertiliser from the government for their tomatoes – did he think the extra tomatoes would be worth the cost? She remained calm with the women but her world, like Fuller's, had been overturned. Used to making her way through the netherworld of Kingston by sensing the wills of others and conforming to their needs, the making of decisions and the holding of responsibility were dizzying exercises in mental application and self-belief. Fuller listened to Regina and was drawn further into Dubeng and its tiny, crippled attempts to move away from poverty. He took his briefcase from where it was covered by cloth – though not sufficiently covered to exclude the dust – bent it open, the dry leather creaking, and found the empty notebook he had expected to fill with his judgements of Kangaba. 'Keep your records in this,' he told Regina. 'Then you will not have to worry about arguments.'

There were victories. Regina could not believe them. They bought a second-hand Singer – which worked – from the border town. The women decided to branch out into making school uniforms. With Fuller in attendance, taking no part but lending weight, the women took their money to the government cooperative store and came back with actual fertiliser. No 'receeps' this time, the women declared with excitement.

A few days after this triumph Regina came to Fuller while he sat at their table, a glass of palm wine by his hand. Her suggestions for buying household items were always carefully rehearsed and staged even though Fuller invariably accepted them. 'Hoo,' she said, 'we should have a tin roof for our house.'

He looked at her, the meaning of this dawning on him.

She continued. 'The thatch has all sorts of insects and little animals. Sometimes bits and pieces fall down and make our bedroom dirty. And it can catch fire too. With a tin roof you do not need to make a new roof every couple of years.'

They had never talked about leaving Dubeng. Neither of them could imagine a future or dared to think of it, though Fuller knew, deep down he knew, the future could not be here.

'Find out how much it will cost,' he replied at last.

'I knows that, Hoo,' Regina replied, pleased with herself. 'I have written it in my book.'

50

Dubeng's koranic teacher was a powerfully built man on the brink of old age. He had a cataract in one eye and seldom smiled, using solemnity, Fuller suspected, to conceal an ordinary understanding. In the koranic school he whipped the boys and refused to teach the girls, but he wrote the words of the Koran in an Arabic script of great elegance using ink and wooden pens he made himself. Fuller had once watched for a full ten minutes while the teacher sat on a mat, a board held between his feet, and laboriously produced in that dusty, approximate place something of perfect form. At that moment he understood the teacher's truculent insistence that it was Islam and not the West which represented the promise of civilisation. When Kamara returned from his second absence, Fuller told him of the teacher's promise to recount the history of Dubeng. Kamara groaned. 'Oh, my god, I'm sorry for you. I'm sorry for me. Listening to that man is like having a termite in your ear. It just bores away.'

The teacher made his presentation one evening on the bantaba. Conversation was usually a fluid affair with give and take, no one claiming absolute authority, but on this occasion the teacher spoke alone and stood while the others sat. Kamara's translation was free and irreverent, sometimes condensing, to the teacher's impotent suspicion, whole minutes of speech into a couple of sentences.

'Oh yes, he wants to go back to the Alkalo's great-great- – too many greats – grandfather – the founder of the village. Actually he's giving you the man's name but you needn't bother with it. My god, I've heard this story so many times. Anyway at the time this man was living far away in the east, in what is now Mali maybe. It was about four hundred years ago. He is giving you the exact years in the Islamic calendar – I don't think that will help you. At the time the Fula were very war-like and wanted to start a new kingdom and make everyone Moslems. At the time our ancestors followed their own religion – actually they still do, but never mind. He is saying that on this occasion the Fula were strong and the Mandinka were not ready so our founder had to flee with his family. They met the river and travelled down it to the present site of Dubeng – the name means shade, or sanctuary. Oh yes, now he is talking about their adventures, how brave they were and so on, how they nearly didn't make it. In those days there were no other villages in this area, there wasn't a village over there or over there. Just forest. The family nearly died again. They were farmers but for the first year they had to fish and hunt. At one time a group of hunters from a tribe downstream discovered them and wanted to kill them but they escaped by canoe. Anyway they survived as you can see and the land which they claimed is still in his family's hands and anyone else who wants to farm here has to have their permission. Yes, that's true. It's interesting. They don't think of it that way, but actually it is a class society. If you come from the ruling family you have rights that the other villagers don't have.

'OK, now he's on the really boring bit. He's telling us how Dubeng came to be a Moslem village. He is telling you the names of all the marabouts who visited the village and what was learned from each one. Yes, he's saying that because of the village's conversion it became the centre of things. Farmers from Dubeng became traders and travelled far north into the desert. Some even crossed the desert to Egypt and Mecca on pilgrimages. A camel route passed nearby – it still does – and people from Dubeng visited other Moslem states, eventually joining with other Mandinka and Fula villages in the region to form their own Moslem state of Bondu. Bondu has its own history but he doesn't want to teach you that tonight. You are lucky; our teacher has a narrow mind which only goes straight ahead. He wants to tell you about the koranic school. It was the school which really made Dubeng's reputation. Dubeng became known as a devout village and the children of other villages came here to learn and to take the message back to their parents. The school taught everyone to read and write, which was a strange thing for most people. Actually, this is true. Most of the men here can write Mandinka in Arabic script as well as being able to copy out the Koran in Arabic. But you know the trouble – nothing in Kangaba is printed in Arabic script. Now he's boasting about the bravery of the village when the English and the French came. Many people were killed fighting the invasion and the Moslems of the north fought much harder than the people in the south.'

The exposition had lasted nearly an hour and the other villagers began to show small signs of impatience, murmuring about the sharing of tobacco and even getting up to attend to some task back in their compound. The disturbances made the teacher lose his rhythm and his facts seemed to become more random. He asserted, according to Kamara, that Dubeng was still a good village. The people worked hard. The koranic school was still famous. Even when the other villages were hungry Dubeng had enough to eat. The women had many skills. Because of the Alkalo's ancestors the village had more river-bank land than their neighbours. And they had fish. 'He's running down,' reported Kamara and he said something in Mandinka which caused laughter.

The teacher did not smile. 'Oh I've upset him. I said the river also gave us smuggling. Now he wants to give me a lecture. He says that the people on the other bank of the river came from the same clan and that we traded together for hundreds of years before the British and the French gave us the border. Apparently we are bound by a common interpretation of the Koran, so smuggling by canoe is all right.'

The teacher went to talk again but, by consensus, the men on the bantaba seemed to have decided that politeness had already been extended to the measure of the man's importance and they began to banter among themselves, make jokes and stretch as if to free themselves of the dust of these old stories. Fuller, though, leaned back against the trunk of the cotton tree and, captivated in spite of Kamara, tried to imagine when the tree had been part of a forest with a single family trying to make a home by it. He imagined those who left two hundred years ago to travel overland three thousand miles to Egypt, or even on to Mecca, with little idea of what they would find. He imagined, too, how the British soldiers must have seemed, each carrying a gun, each carrying ideas about godless savages which the villagers could not have guessed.

51

During these days, as habit made a sort of calm and he came to love Regina, Fuller began to think again of Sheila. She had hardly entered his mind during the first weeks while he was initially distressed and then throwing himself into Dubeng life. Now she returned, like a musical refrain which had always been there, though unheard, beneath the greater noise. It was not the same as before. Instead of reaching back to a remembered Sheila, his last point of contact with his own world, she emerged gently in his thoughts in a sort of rhythm with Regina. He had forgotten how, in the early Oxford days, he had been pleased to stay awake next to Sheila's sleeping body to enjoy its presence more. There had been nights in Oxford when, between making love, Sheila had talked immoderately of her hopes and plans for them and had then been quietly entranced as Fuller had explained his theories of the world. Regina's chatter, her calls on his wisdom, brought these memories back to him. Loving Regina, he relived loving Sheila and in his thoughts he no longer explained to her or demanded explanations, or accused, or apologised. Rather than reviewing the twenty years that had been driven between them, he spoke to her directly as they had spoken twenty years before. He wanted to share with her his unexpected rediscovery of delight.

Dear Sheila . . . He talked to her while he hacked at the guinea-corn with a curved knife, the rustling of its dry leaves blocking out all other noise and showering him with dusty fragments which stuck to his perspiration. Dear Sheila, I never imagined this. Without looking for it I seem to have been given a new life. It's odd to have found it here in a peasant village – I never imagined a poor village might be anything more than the sum of its problems. It was as if, he confided to Sheila, his mind had turned over and he had been offered a clean surface on which to write a new life. It was almost that his old way of looking at the world had been upside down and that the feeling of freshness comes from giving up the effort of living the wrong way round. After all, he argued, more of the world lives in peasant villages than in towns and always has.

Little by little Fuller had been drawn into village concerns. From Regina he had learned of Binta's anxieties. The young man she loved could not afford to marry her and her father might give her instead to old Amadu to be a 'baby nurse' wife for his declining years. This, Fuller was now convinced, was at the centre of life. This and the question of whether, if Binta did succeed in marrying her young man, her brothers would agree to redistribute their father's land in a way which would enable the couple to feed themselves and a family. This was at the centre of life. This and what he learned at the bantaba about the stealing of two goats by unknown people and the attempted murder by bow and arrow of a suspect from a neighbouring village – a dangerous development reviving old grievances. This, and the rains. And the threat of a pestilence of tiny birds which might eat the rice crop before it was in, causing fearsome hardship. Behind the centre, going deeper and deeper, Fuller came to sense the years before, the knowledge of past disasters, the recipes for herbal remedies passed down by mouth from father to son, mother to daughter, old precedents for the use of land, ritual practices which had proved effective in the past. Fuller had come to accept in a month or two that news of a wandering marabout still miles away across an international border was sensible cause for a flurry of excitement and that a string of successes in village wrestling matches was a just basis for a regional reputation and rich rewards.

He sought the words to say all this, wanting to offer his revelation to the young Sheila as a gift, the way he used to tell her of his hopes. Dear Sheila, you see, in England our world was always the town, the countryside was something at the periphery which we rewarded well for supplying us with food and into which we could dip for refreshment. But in Kangaba it is the town which is on the periphery, at the edge, a dangerous barbarity which, unable to satisfy itself, reaches out with a restless greed and cruelty into the helpless countryside and takes what it can. It takes its wealth, its food, its young. When trickery is insufficient it uses force. Negotiation is never equal. When I look back and think how I made these people my business, I am ashamed. I was a buccaneer outside decent society. It makes me humble that Dubeng has taken me in and Regina shares my life. There was only Sheila to tell and he only told her in his mind.

52

On the bantaba, in the evenings, Fuller learned more about 'the project'. Kamara, always stirring, had told them that it was Fuller's employers who were behind it all – people unimaginably far away. This was the nature of the world, Kamara told them. They should learn how they were exploited. It was not the local government employees who were their enemies: they were only puppets.

The project – they always used the English word when they talked of it – was a major landmark in village history, like a war or a flood. There was before the project and after it. Fuller knew the type; it was a routine way for international lenders to invest in the agriculture of peasant countries. A region was selected from a map and, by building roads and introducing farmers to modern agricultural inputs, the produce available for export and to feed the towns was increased. They cost, say, between twenty and fifty million dollars over five years and you usually needed a foreign manager. Fuller knew the type; if he had been doing his job he would have checked the returns on investment.

Before the project, according to the men at the bantaba, things were well in Dubeng. There were always the taxes of course, but like the rains their vicissitudes were familiar. They hardly saw government officials, who did not like to leave the town and who, anyway, did not have the means to do so. The villagers got nothing back for their taxes but for all time it had been so, that the town stole from the villages. On the whole, the men agreed, it was better that the government people left them alone.

The first they knew of the project was the arrival in Dubeng of two big Land Rovers containing officials, politicians and one white man, who was their leader. In all the history of Dubeng they had never received so many important visitors. If they had known they would have provided food and dancing for them – perhaps if they had done so the project would have treated them more kindly. This proposition was discussed at length but on the whole it was rejected.

The white man, they discovered later, came from a place called Italy and had a very long name which no one could remember. They only saw him once but felt his presence for years. He was a powerful man, not as tall as Fuller but fatter, and had a big voice. He promised them everything. He would give them money. There would be miraculous seeds and chemicals which would give them two or three times the harvest for no more effort. There would be a new road to take them into town. People would come to stay in the village and teach them things. He would send them tractors so they would no longer have to strain their backs. They would sell their extra produce to the government and with the money they could buy everything they wanted.

After the group left, the village was for days in a state of shock and confusion. A few advertised their modernity by claiming that the future had come to meet them and they should embrace it. Some said they should resist the invasion at all costs or they would be destroyed and diverted from Moslem ways. The consensus was that they should accept whatever the project gave them but refuse to do what they were told. It was generally agreed, however, that the most probable outcome was that they would hear no more of it.

The first sign that something was happening was the construction of a new road through the area by huge yellow machines. This road, which still existed, was curious because it avoided all the villages and ended up nowhere. It was a mystery but it did no harm. The second sign was the arrival of the 'night clerks'. They called them night clerks because they were very lazy during the day but were active at night creeping around the huts of girls. The villagers were told by the District Officer that they had to accommodate the two young men who, in return, would teach them how to farm. But the young men were from the town and had never farmed in their lives, so how could they teach the people of Dubeng? The night clerks quickly became so embarrassed that they avoided the village men and concentrated on what really interested them – the girls.

After that things got worse, they became really serious. It seemed to start well. One day all the men were told to go to the border town to be given money by the project cooperative – of which, they were informed, they were now members. At last, said the optimists, our virtue is rewarded and what we have paid in taxes will be returned to us. Don't be fools, replied the cynics, it must be a trick. As it turned out nobody was sure at the end of the day as to which view was justified. Yes, they had been given money, but as soon as they received it and had stamped a piece of paper with their thumbs, the money had been taken back again: we opened our hands and the money flew back to its nest like a bird. In return they were given all sorts of seeds and chemicals. They were also told that Dubeng would be sent a big tractor which would plough the rice swamps for them. The men said they were happy at this for the sake of the women – who had not been invited to town – who every year became exhausted digging the rice swamps and suffered from leeches on their legs, and every year somebody lost a wife because of snake bite.

The new seeds were not a success. It might have been that they were received too late, or perhaps it was because the villagers were ignorant about how to use them. On the whole they tended to believe that Dubeng had a special sort of land which only suited the crops which their forefathers had learned to grow there. How can a man from Italy hope to understand farming in Dubeng? In any case it was a bad year and the men who did best were those who took the gifts but refused to use them. The new guinea-corn dried up in a period without rain and the foreign ground-nut had a disease which the village had never seen before.

This was not the worst of it. The women postponed the preparation of the rice land until the arrival of the big tractor. At first they were scared it would not come to the village at all but after the Alkalo went to the town and paid extra money to the driver he did come to Dubeng. All the rice swamps were ploughed in a single day. The villagers saw the power of machinery for the first time. None of the women would have anything to do with the project rice seed – they are less brave than the men – and the rice crop was not bad for a generally poor year. The women liked the tractor and hoped it would come again.

Next came an unexpected visit to Dubeng by the District Officer and their MP – a man they had not seen before. They talked to the villagers very roughly, saying that the people of Dubeng had behaved badly and that it was people like them who prevented progress in the area. The project had given them many good things to improve their lives but they had done nothing to repay the project. Everyone was shocked; nobody had said anything about repayments. They had nothing to pay back with. How could it be that the project with its big yellow machines making a road to nowhere, with so many cars and motor cycles for its staff and with a big man from Italy in charge could not afford to give Dubeng anything?

They were frightened but as the days passed they relaxed again. It seemed that Dubeng was to be left in peace and the next visitors once again caught the village by surprise. A truck filled with young men appeared, making its way along the narrow track with most of its wheels running over the crops. Everyone agreed that it was a very big truck. Two thugs with guns announced to the villagers that they had been sent by the MP who was going to teach them that they could not cheat the government by failing to pay for the project benefits he had secured for them. The rice, they said, was grown from government seed on land ploughed by a government tractor. It was government rice. The young men went from house to house and from store to store taking any rice they could find. If anyone tried to stop them, he was knocked down.

In all its history Dubeng had not had such a misfortune. As they talked of it with Fuller on the bantaba, the men fell silent as if still needing to ponder its meaning. For days after the rice was taken people had just wandered around confused. Even the time so many huts and fences had burned was not like this, even the big drought which the old men remembered. Without the rice the village could not feed itself until next harvest. And there would be no seed for the next planting. Some men wanted to take revenge and fight, but the enemies seemed so distant and all-embracing that nothing came of it. The night clerks would surely have been killed, except that they ran away on their motor cycles – leaving three pregnant girls behind them.

That year the village changed. It had been a prosperous village but its savings were quickly used up. All the single men and, shamefully, some of the girls went to the towns to look for work and, if possible, send money home. Many never returned. Even married men who had always been proud of their farming in Dubeng were forced to work as farm labourers in neighbouring villages to prevent their families from starving. Many marriages were spoiled that year. But, as Fuller could see, they had worked hard and Dubeng was a good village again where, unlike so many places, people had enough to eat. Now they could laugh at their foolishness.

Fuller had wondered aloud that, after all this, they had welcomed him into their village. They smiled and said that it was different: he had arrived with someone they knew. Of course they had been a bit suspicious but Fuller acted like a humble man and did not pretend to know what he did not know. He had not made foolish promises. He came as an African traveller comes, quietly, begging for hospitality. Fuller replied – and it was the truth – that he had not claimed to know things because when he arrived in Dubeng he really knew nothing. They denied this fiercely but thought his modesty becoming.

The project story came out over time, Fuller reclining on the bantaba, Kamara translating, smiling, provoking the discussion. Only near the end did Fuller reveal that he thought he knew the Italian man who ran the project. In Rome Fuller had been invited to the house of this man for dinner – he had gained an important position in an international organisation on the basis of having managed a big project in Kangaba. Fuller said he had not liked the man – he had too many opinions. The Alkalo had nodded sagely and said it was as it always was in towns: it was not the most worthy but the noisiest man who succeeded.

53

When Kamara returned after his third absence he smelled as if he had not washed for days. He draped an arm over Fuller's shoulder and said only, 'I'm tired, man,' before going to a hut and sleeping for a night and a day.

In the early evening cool Kamara shambled to the bantaba, his chest bare, his hair uncombed, and lay flat out on the platform. 'It's getting hot. Very, very hot,' he said to the stars.

In Kingston his remaining friends had been put in Valley Prison or killed. 'Some of the boys did not know anything. They just talked loud for the show.' Others had fled the city for the countryside leaving behind the disorganised, hopeless protests of the ordinary people. 'People are just throwing themselves on the fire. Dying for nothing. Those men you saw at the literacy class, they are finished now.' In the market there was fighting over rice. A shipload of American rice had arrived but Uncle had divided it among his MPs to keep their loyalty and they were reselling it over the border for hard currency. 'They are desperate to fill their foreign bank accounts these days. They all fear for the future now. There is nothing in the Central Bank and they are fighting each other over crumbs. Nobody believes you bankers are going to save them this time.' At some point on his journey Kamara had lost, or abandoned, his sunglasses and he seemed less sure of his ability to order and re-order the world he saw. 'Do you think the banks can save them?'

In Washington, thought Fuller, Kangaba would be one of twenty files on Schwartz's desk. He couldn't tell Kamara it would receive so little attention. The last entry would be an informal note recording the absence of Fuller's situation report, and a request to Operations to discover the reason why. In the meeting, the men, playing safe, concealing the slightness of their knowledge, would refer to 'events in Kangaba' and talk in metaphors. They should 'hold their fire' and 'wait until the smoke had cleared'. They wouldn't want to 'kick a man when he was down', but they would, of course, have to safeguard the continuity of their investments.

Fuller said he did not know, it would depend. Then he gently asked, prying in a way he had not before, whether there was anybody ready to take over power. 'That's the trouble,' replied Kamara with a return of intensity. 'You are right. We are not ready. You are absolutely right. There is not even an army we can convert!'

Kamara fell back on to the bantaba and it seemed to Fuller, as he watched, that whole worlds were passing beneath Kamara's star-gazing eyes and that a hundred battles were recorded in the flexing and unflexing of his muscles. 'Hugh,' he said suddenly, as if unaware that time had passed, 'there's an Englishman, here in the north. He calls himself Colonel Watson. They say he is training some SDF boys. You can go and see him for us. You can do that. We can't do that.'

54

'Come in. You're Hugh Fuller, aren't you?' Watson balanced dangerously on a stool in the middle of the room, bare chested, hands stretched up to the light fitting, fiddling with its tiny screw. He looked too clumsy for the job, hands too rough and old. Still the voice was fine – Oxford, Fuller thought.

'You can't get people here to do simple jobs like this. I'll probably electrocute myself one day . . . or fall and break my neck. Not everybody would be sorry, mind you.' He made a final lunge. 'Oh bugger it!'

Watson climbed down, a tentative foot first searching for the floor with an old man's concentration. Then he straightened himself, looked at Fuller and gave a quick smile full of lines and charm. 'A drink is in order. Excuse the disarray. I have a houseboy but he's off to an aunt's funeral as usual. Have a wife too, but she couldn't take another tour in the tropics. Couldn't understand why I wanted to come back. She said they really don't like me and I dare say she's right. I've beer or gin and tonic. No ice at the moment. Sorry. We'll take them outside – we've got about half an hour of dazzling sunset over the Futa Jallon hills before the insects bite. Still half an hour is better than none. That's what I tell my wife, but she's not convinced. Have you got a wife, Mr Fuller – or shall I say Hugh? Occupational hazard for men like us, losing wives.' Fuller knew then that Watson was not innocent.

They watched from low easy chairs while the sky turned pink, then red, and bright green disputed with shadow for the forest, darkness winning and bringing with it the first sharp cries of nocturnal animals. Watson talked, hardly looking at Fuller, his chest still bare, small breasts where there had been muscle.

'Excuse me if I chew your ear off, Hugh. I'm stuck up here with two hundred illiterate ragamuffins who are supposed to become the President's élite Pioneer Force. If they ever start fighting I'll be the first one they'll shoot. I'm being indiscreet of course, but I don't get too many English visitors. I knew you might be coming, by the way. They told me on the radio. I got the impression you're out of line, old boy. I'm to pump you for information and tell them exactly what you're up to and who you're with. Orders of chief wog, the President hisself.'

Fuller tensed but did not reply, moving instead to empty the last drops from a bottle of beer into his glass before returning his eyes to the distant margin between red and black, avoiding Watson's look which had been turned towards him.

Watson laughed. 'Oh yes, I'm also to tell you that you've got no business here, you're no longer employed, your visa has been revoked and you're to return to Kingston toute suite. Safe passage assured. I suppose you must be important. They didn't actually ask me to arrest you. You don't want to be arrested do you? No. Well I'm not a bloody policeman anyway. I'll get you another beer.'

Fuller waited alone in the low chair, small under the enormous spread of the sunset, and was suddenly very tired. Dubeng already seemed impossibly far away, Regina and the villagers an unnatural contortion. He knew that Watson would try a new approach when he returned and Fuller was prepared to flirt with his own seduction.

'To be honest, Hugh' – the tone was more intimate – 'I don't give a damn. I'm sixty-three and I retired from the army proper thirteen years ago. I get these little training jobs helping to prop up governments which the Foreign Office deems to be important at the time. They don't actually employ me; they just suggest to a government that they might need me to help with some military aid package. Their hands are clean. They expect me to be loyal of course – to the British.' Watson gave another short laugh. 'This time I think I'm part of the Falklands' package. The QE2 put in at Kingston during the war and our planes used the airport. So we owe Uncle a favour. Him, the Americans, the Chileans, the

French and god knows who else. We'll pay and pay. It's all a bit silly really.

'Frankly, just at the moment I care more about having a good chat with you than doing Uncle Funna's dirty work. I don't know what you've done to cause all this static but I'm sure you've got your reasons and if you want to talk about them, one Englishman to another, I'll respect them. I sense we're allies really. You're obviously an educated man, Oxford maybe – from a good family. Got sent down myself and went to Sandhurst instead. The honourable thing to do. Sometimes I feel a bit bitter about it. I think I'd rather have been an anthropologist or something – really get to know places. All I've managed to do is to collect a house full of knick-knacks.' He waved a dismissive hand towards the room behind them. 'I can't remember where half the stuff comes from.'

Now he turned towards Fuller and talked intently to his profile as if he held his eyes. 'You see we're in the same boat really. I hope you don't mind being lumped with a crass soldier. I mean we kick around the world getting hired here and there for this and that purpose, the old skills of empire without the empire. We never know the whole story. We can never really calculate the effects of our actions. I don't really know why I'm here. We don't have any power; we're just used by those who do. I remember fighting against the Mau-Mau in Kenya. I was sure I was on the right side and I believed in what I was doing. Looking back I don't think I had a clue. Now they tell me that training some of Kangaba's bully boys into an efficient fighting force is a good thing – it will keep a useful country friendly. Damned if I know whether they are right or wrong, whether I'm on the side of the angels or not. Frankly, Hugh, the President seems like an old shit to me. What do you think?'

It was dark now. The first reconnaissance mosquito veered close, drilled Fuller's ear, was smashed on Watson's forearm. Time had suddenly become short. Fuller, deep in the chair, the unaccustomed beers heavy in him, dazed by the off-hand splendour of the sunset and Watson's voice, the twists and turns

186

in his story, had no wish to move. The village seemed no place for him. Watson's talk, though shot through with deviousness, bore more interest than threat.

'Do you,' prompted Watson in the dark, 'have any faith in what you are doing? What is it you are doing actually?'

When he spoke Fuller found his words more slurred than could be explained by the drink. 'Well, nothing much really. I'm just making a trip.'

Watson waited, leaning forward, expectant, receptive, looking at Fuller while Fuller looked at the night. When nothing more was offered, he spoke softly, not loud enough to break the spell. 'Perhaps you had better finish your trip here, Hugh. You can stay. I've got a room.'

Fuller breathed deep, grateful for his large lungs, imagining the oxygen chasing out fatigue. 'Thanks,' he was stiffly polite, 'but I expect people are waiting for me.'

For a moment Fuller feared his arms would not be strong enough to push him clear of the low chair and that he would collapse back into it and reckless confidences. He babbled: 'Thanks for the drinks. I enjoyed meeting you.' And he was up and looking down at Watson, who remained folded, wiry and quizzical in his chair. Fuller's politeness was a desperate thing.

Before he could reach the door, Watson was with him, moving fast and light across the living room. 'I'll have to tell them I've seen you. What shall I tell them?'

'Tell them anything you like.'

'Look Hugh, you're too old for advice, but don't make an ass of yourself. And by the way, I nearly forgot to tell you, it seems that your friend – Jacob Cesay – was arrested a few days ago. They've let him go, but it's not always healthy to be let go. I was to tell you.'

Now, for the first time, Fuller turned to hold his look, and it was Watson's eyes which finally slipped away. 'Thanks.' He sat behind the wheel of the mud-caked Mercedes, parked in the entrance road to Watson's old colonial bungalow.

'Is that a government Mercedes?'

'It is.'

Watson only nodded. He seemed rattled by Fuller's sudden departure, wanting to say more but curbed by prudence.

'Oh Colonel,' Fuller was ready to drive away, 'you were right about Oxford. But my family – it wasn't a good one. Not the way you meant.'

55

Back in Dubeng the children once more covered the Mercedes with palm fronds, but this time Fuller did not expect the fronds to stay in place long enough to turn from green to brown. The rhythm of his days had been broken by the visit to Watson and the knowledge that he had not been forgotten preyed on his mind, leaving him caught uneasily between the village and the town. Regina was quiet, scrupulously maintaining their habits as if to provide a mould for Fuller to conform to when he relaxed. At night she silently massaged his shoulders while he lay awake.

He told Kamara what he had learned from Watson: that, yes, he was training the SDF, that the government was expecting trouble. It was as Kamara thought, yet he was tense when Fuller told him and for once was silent. While Kamara sat on his bed, legs pulled up pensively beneath his chin, Fuller's eyes wandered to an open letter in a childish hand. It was some sort of love letter to Kamara. ' . . . I miss you in my heart . . .' He traced it back to the top of the page where it started, 'Dear Comrade . . .'

'We've got no choice,' said Kamara. 'We've got to fight . . . Yes, we've got to fight now. This is the time.' It seemed to Fuller that Kamara had not expected the time to arrive.

Early the next morning Kamara left without waiting to say goodbye. There was a note for Fuller which said he hoped to see him in Kingston, Fuller should pass on his goodbyes to Regina. He said Fuller was like his own family to him and, to Fuller's surprise, he signed it 'Love Latif.'

Four days later Fuller sat alone on the bantaba in the afternoon. The village was quiet and Regina was sleeping alone. He was not quite thinking about what he should do next, but neither was any other thought able to occupy his mind. When the two girls freewheeled into the village clearing Fuller acted as the old men had acted when he had first arrived. He looked at their approach without expression until they were close, then raised a hand and called a word of greeting before waiting for them to explain the meaning of their presence.

The girls were unchanged, still hugging each other, still seeming to take great pleasure in the existence of themselves. There was perspiration on their faces, but the smiles denied anything but a temporary imperfection.

'Mr Fuller. We have come to see you, Mr Fuller.'

'You have to go to Latif.'

'We have travelled all the way by bush path to tell you this.'

'Up and down.'

'On our Honda.'

'It's time for action, Mr Fuller.' She gave an ambiguous smile, as if suggesting something delightful.

'They have doubled the price of rice in Kingston. Everyone is crazy.'

'They are going mad.'

'Latif has to know.'

'He has to go to Kingston now. They have to fight.'

'And he is not safe. You have to tell him.'

'You must leave immediately.'

'Your Benz can go.'

'A minister's Benz can go anywhere.'

'He is at the Bama mines on the western border.'

'Your driver will know.'

'They are not safe at Bama mines.'

'Can we say you will go?'

'Mr Fuller, will you go for us?'

'Quickly, in your Benz. So many people want you to go.'

Still the girls smiled. Fuller looked at them. He had never seen them dismounted from their motor cycle.

'I think Mr Fuller will go,' said one to the other.

'Yes, I think so.'

'We would like to stay with you, Mr Fuller.'

'But we have to go. It's not safe for us.'

'No, it's not safe for girls.'

They turned round the little motor cycle and, without waiting for Fuller to reply, puttered softly away along the single-file footpath, the upright girls bouncing gently as the path rose and fell with the shape of ancient farming ridges. One waved with her right hand, the other with her left.

Fuller waited, remaining sitting on the bantaba for a full two minutes before starting on his clean escape.

He shook Regina awake and told her urgently that it was an emergency, he had to leave immediately. Kamara needed help.

'I come with you,' she said from her dreams, out of instinct.

'No, no. You have too many things to do here. But please find M'bayo. Tell him he has to come now. No arguments.' Fuller found an old authority he had never shown Regina. 'I'll have to leave you to explain to the Alkalo. Say I'll be back as soon as I can.'

'Food for the journey, Hoo. I'll make you something.'

'No time Regina, my love. Please just find M'bayo.'

PART IV

56

When he crashed Jacob was driving the car – an ageing grey Mazda – of a man he had never met. The man was a minor Fula politician who had been killed at a rally during the previous selections, at which time his car had been confiscated by the police. The official version according to *Progress*, the government paper, was that the car was proof that Jacob was part of a conspiracy involving a foreign power and the disaffected Fula. It was cheap of them not to use Jacob's own Mercedes.

According to *Flash*, the day after Jacob was released from Valley Prison he was followed home by a pick-up crammed with members of the SDF and their friends, probably drunk. People remembered the menace of their swelling voices as they sang party songs on their journey through town towards Braithwaite Heights. At Jacob's house the thugs cut off the head of his dog with a palm wine tapping knife, broke the windows and doors and took his drinks, stereo and car. One of the leaders who had drunkenly urinated on his shoes made Jacob lick them clean.

Immediately after they left, Jacob put on old clothes, borrowed money from a neighbour and went to the local bus and lorry stop to find transport to the north. He may have planned to return to his village or to escape across the border to Upper Guinea. At the first check-point, just outside Kingston, he was recognised and taken back to the SDF compound. First they sliced off the soles of his feet, the penalty, it seemed, for trying to run away. Later they also cut off the palms of his hands, perhaps because he crawled. The order of what followed was not clear but it included pushing hot iron rods up his anus and quartering his penis into strips with an open razor. He was scalped before they left him, the top of his head cleaved and taken away.

The car crash was half-hearted. Whoever staged it had not understood its point or did not care. Damage to the car was minimal and it was not set alight. Jacob's body was left in the passenger seat.

Nobody believed the government story in *Progress* that Jacob was fleeing the country with his pockets full of gold. Like the car crash the carelessness of the cover story seemed wilful: it implied that the government was sufficiently powerful to be unconcerned by truth and unafraid of scandal. And *Flash* was allowed to speculate on the reasons for Jacob's death without its proprietor being re-arrested or their press being damaged by a further visit of the SDF. It said that the minister's mistake had been to cross the Syrians. Within the government he had been alone in insisting that they too should conform with the IMF's guidelines on the movement of foreign exchange: they should no longer be able to export their profits as they wished, the money should be used to purchase more rice for the poor. Jacob had described to the President an economic model which had first appeared in his Oxford doctoral thesis twenty years before. Inspired by Fuller's visit he had reached back beyond his years in Kangaba politics to something clear and clean – and, in doing so, had convinced the President of his essential alienation – a man who had been away too long. Uncle remembered the white man from the Bank who Jacob had called his oldest friend, a man important then but now disowned and of little consequence. His instincts told him that Jacob had become a man of mixed allegiance and confused purpose who was better disposed of. The Syrians, who paid for Uncle's homes in Europe and for the party funds that financed the SDF, nudged him further until he nodded and looked away. *Flash* noted that Dr Jacob Cesay was the last of the government's technocrats and asked, 'How long can we go on spilling the blood of the best and the brightest of our soil's children?'

While Fuller was listening to Colonel Watson talking about training the ragamuffins of the SDF, Jacob was probably already dead. Certainly he was past the point when he would have wanted to retrieve his life. There had been no conspiracy. The documents that Jacob had passed on to Fuller through Kamara were of no significance, their red ribbons and 'Top Secret' stamps were the ceremonials of a way of doing things that had long become irrelevant. But his old teacher's presence had exercised its pull on Jacob and had led him to a sudden decision, a keeping of faith with a former self, which Fuller's decision to stay had made impossible to forget.

Fuller read the crumpled week-old copy of *Flash* at a petrol station. M'bayo had brought it to him. When Fuller had read the article through and said nothing, M'bayo muttered, 'They done kill him, sir.'

Fuller breathed deep, taking in petrol vapour. The article had not mentioned Fuller, only hinting that Uncle did not like Minister Cesay's closeness to foreign influences. He tried to think of something useful he could do and for a moment his mind turned to the British High Commission before it was torn away from this treachery.

'Sir,' M'bayo broke into his thoughts, 'I want to go home now.' M'bayo had left the keys in the car's ignition, something he never did, his belief in the Mercedes' protection swept away by the news of his minister's death. He edged round until Fuller was between himself and the car. 'Sir, I believe it is dangerous now.'

In his mind Fuller had moved from Jacob to Latif, the horror pushed aside by calculation of what might still be done, who might still be saved. 'How far to the mine now?'

'Not far now, sir. Thirty KMs.' The modern affectation was intrusive.

'Will I get there?'

'You might, sir. They might not stop you . . . Please sir, can I go home?'

'Yes, of course. You should go.' Fuller shook M'bayo's hand. 'You've done well.'

57

On the drive to Bama Mines Fuller offered no words to Sheila. The unfinished sentences, all starting 'Dear Sheila, I . . .' no longer surfaced. His mind was mapped by dashing lines of reason, calculating, testing this alternative against that. The present, the future. No past.

Rain started; the dirt road became slick with silty mud. With the windows closed the car was humid, full of the smell of his own sweat. Fuller filled the space. Unnaturally large raindrops smashed the ground with a force that raised mud into the air, making of the outside an enclosing mood of spray and dirt, which assaulted the car in conspiracy with a storming wind. Fuller no longer drove but manhandled the Mercedes along a road which was only hinted at by the headlights reflected back from this day-time dark. As he became more physical his mind became cooler. If a check-point suddenly loomed, red and white striped pole across the road, the SDF would be sheltering somewhere with their guns under cover. He would have ten seconds, maybe twenty. It would be enough. If the barrier was a pole he would smash through; if it was something heavy, a vehicle perhaps – it was unlikely – he would assess the situation immediately, he would slide the car into a turn. He was certain that he would size up the situation correctly, certain that he would get the manoeuvre right, certain that his wits and abilities could better the thugs'. He could leave the car and take to the bush; they'd never find him in this weather. As he drove he calculated the distance he'd have to run and walk to the camp: ten miles, five. In his mind he ran through the map of the area fixing the physical features he would look for as he made his way through forest and farms. He laughed at old fears of the African bush: the snakes would not awake before his feet moved on. Sweating, in the rain, on the run, nature would take him in, let him pass. Even if the SDF cornered him and questioned him, there was another plan.

He would brazen them, give orders, refer to Colonel Watson by name, pretend to be the Colonel's superior. Those boys could not be sure who a white man was or what might be the roots of his authority. Plans and counter plans contended in his mind while his face stayed firm, his temper cool and his driving wisely judged. Failing all that, as a last resort, if the danger was real, there was the wheel-wrench next to his seat, a piece of heavy metal and Fuller a large and powerful man. He had the confidence, too, that as his arm came down towards the head of some teenage gunman it would not be checked by a sudden rush of liberal reservations or a wish to smile, make friends and confide that he really wasn't serious. His arm would be committed; it would strike a crushing blow, while his mind would have moved already to seizing the gun, keeping low and taking cover before his victim's ill-disciplined comrades could bring their slower reactions to bear.

There were no road blocks. Fuller found the track up to the mining camp first time as he knew he would. There was a wire gate, long broken open and now clambered upon by all sorts of joyful vegetation liberated by the support it offered. The track curled its way up a hill. To the mud and the waves of rain was now added a barrier of tall grass that grew between the two wheel tracks, dense and straight and six feet high. The tracks themselves were only visible as reflections of twin streams rushing towards the car while in between the tall grass stood square in front of the windscreen to be mown down like endless ranks of assembled soldiers, forever promising to reveal some deadly surprise, yet never fulfilling its promise.

And suddenly Fuller was on top of the hill, in a clearing, in the camp. The same momentum which had carried the car up the slippery track and had crashed it through the towering grass now sent it slithering sideways across the slick mud into the gullet of the camp, a low building on each side and a third directly ahead, by which the car finally came to rest at an unintended angle.

Rain poured off the corrugated iron roofs of the blockhouses in shifting waterfalls making a deep trench in the mud and veiling thirty shuttered windows and no sign of movement anywhere. Fuller tested the car but the wheels spun to no effect. He looked around him: there was nothing to show that anyone stayed there, there was no sign of other vehicles discreetly parked, no tyre tracks recent enough to have survived the storm.

The two shutters of the window nearest him opened slowly, noiseless as a film, and then the barrel of an automatic rifle was rested on the sill ten feet from Fuller's head. He could not see the person behind it. He slid over to the passenger seat, keeping his hands visible on the seatback and dashboard affecting an expression between anxiety and a smile and wound down the window.

'Who are you?' came a voice, in English, distant across the rain.

'I'm looking for Latif,' Fuller shouted back. 'I'm a friend of Latif's.'

There was silence. The barrel of the gun moved along the length of the car and back as if it were an eye.

'Move the car away,' commanded the voice. Someone thought it was a bomb.

'I can't. It's stuck.'

Again there was silence. Fuller caught sight of the whites of eyes rising above the sill of the dark room and then dropping down.

At last the voice came again. 'What do you want with us?'

'I've got a message for Latif. My name's Fuller. I'm a friend of Latif's.'

'Get down from the car.'

His feet, when he stepped from the car, sank into the fine mud, which squirmed its way into his shoes, as cold and intimate as plaster. Heavy footed, unable to feel whether or not the suction had claimed his shoes, Fuller took the three steps to the cemented walkway underneath the eaves. 'Stay there!' warned the voice as he moved towards the window.

A second automatic rifle and then a young man with the gun strap round his neck appeared at the corner of the building, while the gun at the window remained aimed at Fuller's chest. The young man wore sandals, flared trousers and a yellow T-shirt from the University of California – UCLA. He looked at Fuller, looked around at the surrounding forest, then back at Fuller. 'Which Latif?'

'Latif Kamara.'

'Who are you to this Latif?'

'I'm his friend. His sisters told me about the camp and asked me to give him a message. I'm a friend of the family.'

'We don't know you. We don't know of any white man. Are you armed?'

'No.' There was no attempt to check.

'Have you any cigarettes?'

Fuller pulled out the packet in his breast pocket and offered them. The young man took the packet, removed two and passed the rest through the window.

'Are you a Marxist?'

Fuller thought. He asked himself seriously whether or not he was a Marxist, to what extent he had a view of the world that could be termed anything, whether it might not be argued that we are all Marxists now, even the most unreflecting anti-communist not completely unaffected by Marx's understanding of the modern world. Then he thought how innocent and sad it was that this young man should test allegiances by such a question, the answer to which must be unreliable, and only after all this, after long seconds of reflection following the busy mind-racing drive, did Fuller consider that his answer might determine his life or death. Then he remembered Oxford and replied, 'I've often been called a Marxist. I suppose you could say I'm a socialist. It depends on the interpretation of Marx.'

'No,' the young man replied firmly, appearing in no way put out by the complexity of Fuller's answer, giving, in fact, the appearance of having participated in many such discussions and by answering Fuller giving him a measure of acceptance. 'No, what you say is not true. There are only two interpretations of the world – capitalist and Marxist – the rest is irrelevant.'

He would have continued but was interrupted by a voice speaking in another language from inside the building. 'My comrade wants to know,' he translated, 'whether you have been to Latif Kamara's, home.' Fuller said he had. 'Tell us, then, something only a friend would know.'

'He keeps,' offered Fuller after thought, 'chest expanders under his bed and uses them every morning when he gets up and every evening before he sleeps.'

The voice inside the building spoke again and Fuller's interrogator again translated. 'He says that what you say is true. But he also says that the police would know that too.'

'Oh, come on!' Fuller let himself laugh. 'Do you really think that if I was with the police I would come here like this on my own?'

'No, I do not think that.' There was a moment when a smile was almost there, almost shy.

'Please,' Fuller became business-like, 'let me talk to Latif. What I have to say may be important. He will vouch for me.'

'Latif is not here. We too would like to talk to Latif.' He reached into Fuller's shirt pocket for matches and lit a cigarette.

Now others appeared, leaving the buildings by invisible rear doors and trickling round the corners to crowd under the eaves, pushing up to Fuller or observing him from a distance. Some clustered around the car, ignoring the rain. They tried to open the boot and before they used force, Fuller shouted out to tell them how. In all there were perhaps a hundred young men, mostly teenagers. None had uniforms and the style of dress was that of the urban poor: colourful, cheap, worn, poorly made in the Western style, the T-shirts advertising a dozen commercial products or foreign causes about which the wearers were unaware or did not care. Fuller saw only the two guns – AK47s he thought. The boys – the guerillas – looked unhappy. Some affected anger that he had brought no food. They pushed Fuller a little. They had been waiting for a fight and were angry that it should have been Fuller that arrived, offering so slight a focus for their anger. Fuller's interrogator calmed them when necessary; he seemed to have some sort of authority. He translated his talk with Fuller into languages the others could understand to ease their suspicions. To Fuller he confided, 'I'm the Political Officer. I've been to the German Democratic Republic and to Libya. I want to discuss Marxism with you,' he added almost gaily amidst the grim and restless mood.

'Where is Latif?' asked Fuller.

'We don't know. He should be here. He should be back from Libya.'

'Libya?'

'Yes they're our friends. You did not know that?' The question was sharp.

'Oh,' lied Fuller, 'I knew Latif had contact with the Libyans. I didn't know he went there.'

The young man did not press him. Instead there was a blank statement made with his eyes averted. 'We've got no food. Our guns haven't arrived yet. We are going crazy waiting to know what to do.'

While Fuller took this in the Political Officer's face underwent a dramatic change: his jaw fell and his eyes enlarged, staring at the clearing behind Fuller's head with a terrible anxiety. The noise of the assembled guerillas diminished and disappeared as classroom voices quieten on the entry of the most feared schoolmaster. The last words of the last speaker still hung in the rain. Fuller turned with the others. In the centre of the clearing, dark brown, duller than the mud, had appeared an armoured car, its turret closed. Not a big armoured car, a small fry in the wars which are seen on film and television screens, but in the clearing it was as high as the single-storey buildings and by far the hardest and most deadly thing in view. It had no markings. No one moved. Two little machine-guns mounted on its front made jerky, robotic movements, demonstrating that the guerillas on all three sides were within their range.

Nothing happened. The armoured car sat squat and still,

matched by its mirror-image on the surface water, the rain pouring down on it. No one addressed it, asked whether it was friend or enemy. The turret did not lift an inch to give an indication of enclosed humanity. Its big gun pointed exactly at Fuller's Mercedes and the place behind it where Fuller stood next to the Political Officer, who had managed one crazed, questioning glance at Fuller before he was, like the others, struck dumb and still.

After minutes, a knot of nudging boys at the extremity of the buildings, unravelled and began to slip away towards protection. A machine-gun twisted and clacked urgently above the tin roof clatter of the rain, taking its line, cutting down two boys that Fuller could see, producing flying lumps of plaster and concrete from the walls, making to collapse like dominoes the crowded inhabitants of that wing, some running forward towards the armoured car only to run back. Their shouts were silenced by the gun, which, after it had stopped firing, after five or six were dead or wounded, continued its movement along the line, passing wild minds which could not discern for sure whether the gun was alive or dead, whether they were hit or spared.

When the voice came from the armoured car it was enormous and mechanical, an amplification system for crowd control. Fuller thought, though he could not be sure, that the voice was English – upper class and English. It said: 'Release the white man.'

Fuller wanted to assert his solidarity, his wish to be associated with the guerillas, but he saw no way, only the prospect of antagonising the occupants of the armoured car. He was not held; he walked freely towards the voice, becoming drenched, the hundred pairs of eyes now on him.

'No! Get into your car.'

Fuller turned back and slid behind the wheel of the Mercedes, its door left open. He did not want to leave; he was certain there was to be a massacre.

'Drive to the main road,' said the voice. 'Report there.'

Now Fuller wanted to make clear to the guerillas that the

inference was wrong, he was not under command. He had no connection with the armoured car. He stood up again, square opposite the barrel of the main gun. 'The car's stuck. It won't go,' he screamed at the unmoved metal. 'What do you want? I want to know who you are.'

'Get back into your car, Mr Fuller.' The machine-guns twitched to show their alertness, that their attention had not been distracted. 'Now! Please!'

Fuller returned to the driver's seat.

'Push the car.' One of the machine-guns, a deformed little arm, gestured at the group of guerillas nearest to Fuller. Half a dozen came forward, surrounded the car, began to push. Fuller turned on the engine. Next to Fuller's face, separated only by glass, strained by effort, strained by terror, was a boy's face, the face of someone who Fuller was sure was about to die. The Mercedes unglued itself from the mud, started to move. 'White bastard!' hissed the boy. 'White bastard!'

58

At the Sun Hotel on the Kingston beach, it was Hawaiian Night for the holiday-makers. Red and yellow fairy lights illuminated by the hotel's own generator were strung around the pool and the Kangaban musicians made a gesture towards someone's idea of Hawaiian music. The French management had supplied them with bright shirts. Fuller's escort – a Scotsman, he thought – took a key from the bow-tied receptionist and passed it to Fuller, then left without a word to either.

The young Scot, in a uniform which betrayed no rank, had spoken little on the journey back to Kingston, only swearing in a self-contained way at the weather and the muddy road. He drove the Mercedes fast but awkwardly, leaning tensely forward close to the wheel. He was slight and fair yet there was something in his manner which made Fuller think of a leathery countryman who had turned out to rescue some damn fool holiday-maker. Fuller imagined that the younger man despised him and had no time for someone who did not know his place and should know better.

When they were stopped at a SDF check-point ten miles outside Kingston the soldier rolled down his window and without waiting to be addressed transferred his swearing from himself to the approaching gunmen. In spite of his slightness he showed no self-doubt in telling them to 'move the fucking barrier' and to 'stop poncing up and down with your fucking toy guns and get moving.' The SDF boys caught the tone and stopped their advance, turning slack-jawed to roll aside the concrete-ballasted oil drums, one even offering an ingratiating smile as he was brushed aside by the accelerating car. The Scot seemed vaguely cheered by the encounter and by the time they reached the

Kingston outskirts had given up swearing in favour of a grimly toneless medley of songs from before his time. 'She walks like an angel', sounded vindictive, 'All I want to do is fall in love', sarcastic. He used the horn repeatedly and unnecessarily as if the road was filled with its normal swarm of pedestrians instead of being deserted.

There had been two military Land Rovers at the bottom of the hill outside the guerilla camp and Fuller's escort had stepped down from one of them. He gestured that Fuller should move over and took the driving seat without explanation. He seemed to have his orders.

Fuller attempted conversation, trying to conceal his horror at the killing he had seen and the worse killing which he now imagined. He wanted to remain his own man, engaged and wily. 'Where are we going?' His tone was even.

The young soldier looked sharply at Fuller as if surprised that he could talk. 'Kingston.' He turned back to his driving.

Fuller pressed on. 'I didn't understand what was happening up there. What's going on?'

There was no reply. A pot-hole concealed by water jarred the car and got a sworn response. 'Fucking cart track.'

Fuller considered asking what was the British involvement, what regiment did the soldier belong to, but he rejected the questions as provocative. Instead he chose: 'Why were those boys being arrested?' Again there was no reply and Fuller added, 'It might be better if I knew the official version.'

The soldier glanced across at Fuller a second and final time, sceptical and uninterested, then, after driving on for a while, he offered: 'Teach the fucking monkeys a lesson.'

Instead of going to the centre of Kingston they turned off early along the road which passed over Braithwaite Heights before dropping to the beach and the Sun Hotel. Fuller could see smoke rising from several parts of the city and thought he could hear sharp bursts of automatic gun-fire. 'Catch a falling star. Put it in your pocket,' Fuller heard his companion tersely instruct himself as they curved down the drive to the entrance of the hotel, where a uniformed doorman stepped forward to open Fuller's door.

59

The hut was cemented and perfectly round. A double bed was built-in on top of a fibre-glass base, its white sheets were fresh and already turned back, stretched tight across a corner. On the pillow was a red flower and an advertisement for Hawaiian Night – every Thursday. For the women guests grass skirts could be obtained from the management, Hawaiian shirts for the men. 'Remember South Pacific . . .' went the blurb. Fuller read it at arm's length and placed it aside on top of the room service menu and a brochure for car hire, then lay flat out on his back, his arms above him. What now? He smelled of sweat, the creases in his white shirt were marked out by the dust like tie-dye cloth. His ankles were hardly distinguishable from his shoes, both still caked in the dried red mud from the guerilla camp. There was a moment when he nearly rested and when rest could have become repose and repose, reflection, but Fuller caught the slyness of the moment and before it could have its way he flexed himself and stood away from the bed, unwilling, yet, to be outside the game. He would shower. He should eat.

By the time Fuller joined the tourists on the patio of the swimming pool it was evening. There was no sign of trouble in Kangaba. People laughed. Fuller joined the queue for food at one of the barbecues. He strained to listen for gun-fire above the noise of the Hawaiian music but could not be sure. He wondered if he was a prisoner, whether he was watched. On the stage there was a contest among the tourists for the best imitation of native dancing. There were Germans, French, English, a few Americans. The musicians kept their smiles fixed while a fat French woman, who maybe once knew how to dance, rotated her hips in a proud imagined professionalism. An English girl, red shoulders peeling from the sun, got cheers when, during her dance, a breast momentarily escaped her bikini top. She put it away, laughing, hardly embarrassed – on the beach all the tourists went topless in Kangaba. Fuller took mango, pineapple, paw-paw, steak, sausages, chicken, rice, baked potatoes in silver foil, grilled fish, a mess of stewed vegetables. The servers behind the table in their high cooks' hats, smiled, did not seem surprised. They were used to greed.

The table Fuller chose was in the most distant corner, under a palm tree and illuminated only by a string of coloured lights. Nearer the band the holiday-makers had started to dance with each other. Some were drunk. A woman in a filmy dress, breasts visible – an Italian Fuller thought – sashayed close to him and then away. A married woman on holiday testing the strength of her charms.

'Sir,' said a waiter. 'Can I find you a Hawaiian shirt? I have one that will make you look very handsome.' Then the waiter dropped his smile abruptly and brought his head close to Fuller's. 'Do I know you, sir?'

Fuller looked at him but could not remember. He had met so many young men.

The waiter drew back his head. 'No. I'm sorry. I think I am making a mistake.' He went to walk away then changed his mind. 'Do you know one Regina?'

'Yes, I know her.' Fuller spoke slowly, holding the waiter's eyes. 'Are you a friend of Regina's?'

'Yes. You remember me.' It was an assertion rather than a question, as if being forgotten was unthinkable. 'I was at the Paradise Gardens. Now I am here.'

There had been a young man who cooked the chickenburgers at the Paradise Gardens and Fuller now saw it was him. He offered his hand which was warmly taken then, on second thoughts, quickly dropped.

'I hope my sister is fine.'

'She was fine two days ago.'

The waiter nodded, now completely serious, his mind not on these formalities. He looked around the hotel, then spoke low.

'So many people want to know about you. Your friend . . .' He looked hard at Fuller and Fuller nodded.

'I'm coming.' The waiter edged away nervously. 'You're staying here isn't it? Alright, I'm coming.' He walked away briskly, ignoring loud calls for service from other tables. As he passed, he touched the elbow of a fellow waiter who fell into step behind him.

More than an hour passed before the waiter returned. When he came he brought a bottle of cold beer to Fuller's table and slipped beneath it a folded scrap of brown paper. Fuller drank the beer and took the paper to his chalet.

The message read: I beg you to help us. Please follow this boy at your earliest convenience. Amie Kamara.

Someone had helped her write it. Her name was signed in Arabic script with the Roman version in clerkly parentheses below it.

The footpath was well used. It started behind the hotel kitchens and left the hotel grounds through a flap in the wire fencing. A steep slope – Fuller could not have managed it so easily before his stay in Dubeng – led to a cluster of huts which might have been a small fishing village, or perhaps a community entirely parasitic on the hotel kitchens. They skirted this settlement and, following his guide blindly in the dark, Fuller soon found himself in an outlying area of Kingston old town, a place where village mud buildings mixed with shacks made from the refuse of the city, where people made do with crumbs while they waited for the city to give up its riches to them. 'Curfew,' warned the boy, his Hawaiian shirt conspicuous in the shadows. 'We will avoid the road. It's OK.'

They moved from compound to compound, sometimes passing through the living rooms of houses – the occupants shocked then friendly, astonished to see Fuller – sometimes squeezing down the narrow alleyways between compound walls. Gun-fire was sporadic following no pattern that Fuller could detect. Once it was so close that their ears rang, but they could not see who fired the gun and after a minute crouched over a sewerage ditch they moved on, nervous now. The first body they passed was in a ditch; in a street they saw half a dozen more. 'There is a real battle. I think our freedom fighters must have stolen guns from the SDF armoury.' Fuller peered at the bodies of dead boys but could not see one with the red beret of the SDF.

'You know this place?'

Fuller could not imagine that in all this irregular complexity there might be anything familiar. His attention had not left the back of the guide who drew him through it. Now he peered out through the gateway of a wall across a deserted, dirty street. At last he recognised the neat whitewashed wall and metal gate of the house that Kamara's aunt had built. 'Kamara's house?'

The boy nodded. 'I must go now.' He left without offering the chance of discussion.

Fuller waited in the dark, completely alone, completely out of place. He was in the gateway of a compound and could not tell whether or not the shuttered rooms behind him were empty. The wall next to him had been hit by bullets from an arcing automatic gun, surprisingly large pieces removed by each impact. Two bodies of young men were embracing the dirt of the road to his left. All was still until a single boy with an automatic rifle sauntered past the intersection beyond the bodies, looking around him without any sign of guile or anxiety. Fuller could not tell whether he was SDF or not and in a moment of mental panic found he could not calculate whether a solitary white man would be safer with the SDF or a rioter.

The boy seemed to look at Fuller but walked on without hesitating. As far as Fuller could tell most of the gun-fire was coming from the government office and modern shopping district somewhere behind him. The gate to Amie Kamara's compound on the other side of the wide road was closed, the single small window facing the road shuttered. Now he could see that there were bullet marks in the whitewashed walls – the marks were probably smaller because of the bricks she used to build it, he thought irrelevantly, trying to affirm a local knowledge.

Fuller was suddenly and completely terrified of being killed by a bullet. The forward momentum that had brought him this far was abruptly taken from him, leaving him stationary, poised, exposed, with only useless reason returned to him. A grown man, not young, supposedly wise, in this foreign place, in the street, in this crazy hopeless situation. All at once he wanted to fight with himself, beat the dumb stupidity into submission.

The boy with the gun who had sauntered past now returned, walking backwards. He looked towards Fuller and Fuller's once white shirt. He raised his gun, not quickly, not high, and Fuller took time to connect this easy movement with bullets, with death. He stepped back behind the wall, his slow reaction chased by the impact of bullets around him, the loudness of the gun's report. The wall flung sharp fragments at him, rice at a wedding thrown by a hostile relative. He sank to his knees, was unhurt. He formed the words then made himself murmur, 'Holy shit!' His legs were shaking. He listened very hard for approaching footsteps but heard none. But you wouldn't on the dusty road. At last he dared to look out, expecting a gun-barrel at his head. He could not see the boy. He dared a longer look. The road was empty. Then deciding, then not deciding, then discovering that he was already on his way, he ran across the street to the door of Amie Kamara's house, battering noisily on the corrugated iron door, shouting out, 'Open! It's me! Fuller!' He turned his back to the door scouring the street with his eyes, exposed everywhere. It was still. Flames reached high from the shopping district. A bolt was pulled back and the door scraped over the ground. At first Fuller could not see anyone but when he looked down he found the serious face of the little girl who had fetched the bottles of Fanta on his first visit.

Amie Kamara was in her high bed, in repose. She inclined her head in welcome and almost smiled, but her face was swollen,

213

bruised out of symmetry, maybe broken. 'Sit down,' she said softly in English. 'Police,' she added, again in English, showing him her face. Then she talked in her own language and the child, flustered at her prominence, her own English not good, translated. It was an apology. But for her injuries she would have come to Fuller.

Her first question, deathly soft, was a single word. 'Latif?'

'I think he is safe. I think he is in Libya.'

The child had difficulty with Libya and made of it something the aunt could not believe. 'Not in Kangaba,' added Fuller.

'Not in Kangaba?' She repeated the words.

'Yes. Not in Kangaba.'

She was quiet for a time. When she spoke again Fuller had to remind the child to translate – she could not understand the necessity of it. Then, 'Do his friends come to Kingston to help us?'

'No. I think they will not come.'

'Can you help us?'

'No.'

'Finish!' the aunt breathed quietly in English, then added something else, something final.

'She say, people dead for nothing.'

'Yes.'

Again there was a long silence. When she spoke it was in short sentences to help the little girl translate. 'She say, sorry no Fanta.' Then, 'She say, thank you for coming.' Then, 'She say you are brave. You are a friend. She say, be at peace.'

By the morning it was over, people were in the streets. Fuller left the house and took a taxi to the Sun Hotel. The receptionist stared but said nothing. In his hut he fell on the bed and slept.

There was someone in his room. The voice seemed sure it belonged but the whole world passed through Fuller's mind before he recognised it as Colonel Watson. 'Heard you were here. Thought I'd drop in on you.' He seemed dapper, in good form. 'Tea at the British High Commissioner's house. Nicest house in Kingston. You can clean up there. He may even be able to lend you a clean shirt. No arguments old chap. Let's go.' He acted like an old friend being a good friend.

60

The High Commissioner's house overlooked the sea, one of the houses from the old days which the British had quietly hung on to. Its garden was magnificent, high flowering shrubs nearly concealing the building from the road, its extent further obscured by the steep hill-side which meant that only the highest of three tiers was visible from the front, the third and lowest tier being flush with the cliff edge, sliding glass doors making of it a garden or a reception room by choice. Worn wooden steps reached down the low cliff to the beach.

'You see,' observed Colonel Watson, guiding Fuller through the rooms as if he was the host, 'these Foreign Office types do themselves all right. Never mind all this talk of cuts.'

The High Commissioner, a small podgy man whose suit trousers were supported by comfortable braces with nearly a clown's looseness, greeted Fuller with a mixture of warmth and diplomatic embarrassment. 'I think we can sit outside. I've asked for a sort of buffet. I didn't know whether you had eaten, Mr Fuller.'

Quiet servants who knew their job set up three chairs, a table of dishes. One whispered a question in Fuller's ear. 'To drink, sir?'

'Whisky,' replied Fuller. 'On its own.'

In front of Fuller an abundance of purple and pink flowers tumbled over the cliff edge; above them was the blue of the sea. Too bright, too blue. A mature garden, thought Fuller, remembering the argot of Newbury estate agents. Jacob's house further down the coast had been expensive enough, but bare. There had not been enough time for landscaping. Remembering Newbury, remembering Jacob, remembering Sheila, Fuller closed his eyes. What now, what now?

'It's remarkable how everything grows in Kangaba,' offered the High Commissioner. 'Incredibly fertile. It should be the garden of Africa really. A great tragedy.'

Fuller's whisky arrived. White wine was resting in a silver ice bucket – something valuable, old, something from another time. The tureens, too, were spotless and antique. Little flames, cunningly contrived, kept the food hot, survived the breeze. The High Commissioner picked up and rang a hand bell to call a servant. He chuckled, turned to Fuller. 'It's a bit of an anachronism but actually it seems to be the system that works best. The servants like it.' The High Commissioner wore his plumpness well, as if his fat was made from air.

'Well it's over then,' said Watson, lifting his glass. 'Nasty while it lasted.' He drank.

The High Commissioner, nearly bald, nearly comic, seemed to strain for thoughtfulness, perhaps wanting to set his profundity against Watson's perkiness. 'Yes, these urban food riots are a bad business. I was in Egypt of course during the riots there. Our riots pale into insignificance by comparison. Still on balance I'm inclined to think they might not be a bad thing. Don't you think so Mr Fuller? They release the pressure and remind these tin-pot dictators that the poor are still with them. It's when they get political that they really get nasty. When they get organised. Then you get a real blood-bath. What do you think, Mr Fuller? Or don't you bank people think in these terms? I suppose it's all economics to you – efficient price policy and so on. I have to say that sometimes I find you fellows a bit narrow.'

The High Commissioner waited for Fuller's reply, showing Watson his shoulder to discourage intervention. Fuller looked at the sea and nursed his drink. A memory of Dubeng and Regina crossed his mind, impossibly distant. He let them go, turned his mind again, picked up a familiar load from where he had dropped it months ago. He knew how. He smiled a little, allowed the mildest twinkle of conspiracy to play behind his eyes. 'Oh, we're not as naïve as all that you know. We occasionally let the real world influence our thinking. It's just our reports we keep it out of.'

'Yes, yes,' chuckled the High Commissioner showing pleasure.

'I think that's how you do it. You use the knife but you never show it. You keep it under your economic cloak. You work in mysterious ways. I'm not sure that a classical education is such a bad preparation for divining the world even in these days of you economic theorists. Not that you don't seem to have got your hands dirty a bit this time. My goodness, your people couldn't begin to work out what you were up to. Well, perhaps we shouldn't look too closely. Less said the better.' He was relaxed, jovial. 'We all have to break out now and again. Jolly good thing too. You're back in harness now I take it?' As he asked the High Commissioner nodded his affirmation, not entertaining doubt.

Fuller engaged the High Commissioner's eyes, smiled. 'I feel like I've never been away.'

'Good . . . good. You'll need a break of course. Revolts are tiring, even failed ones. They'll give you a break will they?'

'No problem. I'm freelance. My own man.'

'Yes, can't say I blame you. Wouldn't want to get too tied to the Americans myself . . . Well, Mr Watson,' – not Colonel, Fuller noted – 'are you happy? Will the Americans be happy?'

'Old bastard's still in his palace. All's right with the world.' Watson drank to it. 'Hugh's back in the fold.' Another long drink. 'Out of the cold.'

The High Commissioner nodded, tolerantly, encouragingly. 'Ye-es . . .'

'And I'm getting too old for all this,' Watson concluded.

'Nonsense. You've done a wonderful job. Not an easy place to work, Kangaba.'

'What was it exactly?' Watson, no longer chipper but tired, perhaps drunk, was suddenly earnest, leaning towards the High Commissioner. 'I've been wondering. Was it the harbour? Are they looking for an alternative in case they lose the South African facilities? Is that why they want Kangaba? Or is it uranium? Someone told me that there is uranium in the north. Something else? Can't seem to get a grip on it. Bothers me.'

'Come now. Ours not to reason why . . . Probably it was just out of habit. If I tried to make sense of all my instructions from London, I'd have had an ulcer years ago.' His jolliness denied the world of ulcers. 'Well I'd better go. There's still a good deal of cleaning up to do. And our masters have to know.'

61

Why does the sea have this effect, stroking sadness, deepening it, taking away its dangerous edge? The sea breathed and he visualised its ritual from his long day's watching. Far out where the sand started, the deceitful calm reared into glassy ridges which glided precarious towards the beach, a late deference to gravity. Another crash, a hiss. Kangaba. Fuller stood in front of the plate glass of the British High Commissioner's house, a whisky clasped to his stomach, and stared out into the night. The white of the breakers was just visible; everything else was lost to the yellow reflections of the room. The light from a parchment-shaded standard-lamp dimmed, revived, then dimmed again, the electricity supply not yet quite steady. He recalled that there had been a scandal about the generating plant which he had read in *Flash* a long time ago. The details no longer concerned him. All day he had listened for a renewal of the gun-fire but it had not come. Dear Sheila, he began, and clenched his eyes. Why did the sea have this effect, stroking sadness, deepening it? Perhaps it was only island races that felt this way, perhaps these were the feelings of an Englishman. Dear Sheila . . . and all he had lost. 'The most beautiful country I have ever known,' he muttered aloud, fierce in pushing aside rival claims, adding Kangaba to those he had once loved. He wondered about Regina in Dubeng and could not imagine how she would be without him. He remembered Jacob and wondered about his own part in his death, finally deciding against guilt. Then he thought of Kamara and wondered as to Kamara's fate. He pressed himself closer to the glass to see Kangaba better, to neutralise his image with himself. Again the sea exhaled. He supposed Kamara would be all right.

62

After four days the High Commissioner said, 'You can go back to the Ambassador now. There's someone there to see you.'

'Hello Hugh.'

'Sheila!'

Sheila stood up from the ruined couch where she sat, neat in a sun-dress, her expertly cut short hair unmoved by the passing breeze, and kissed Fuller firmly on the cheek.

'What are you doing here?' He removed her from him gently.

'Visiting you.'

'The kids?'

'I sent them pony-trekking. Anyway they are interested in boyfriends and girlfriends these days, not us. They're getting old you know. They will leave us soon.' She sat again, patting the armchair next to her for Fuller.

He sat down slowly, dizzy, his eyes on Sheila's face trying to discover the meaning of what she said, his slack jaw trying to align itself with Sheila's composed and slightly knowing smile. 'Sheila . . . I never expected this. You've never visited me before.'

'I know . . . I thought it was time. You never asked.'

Fuller nodded slowly, dropping his eyes to the floor of the Ambassador lounge, where the pattern of the tiles was nearly worn away. The grey forelock of his hair, longer now, fell across his face, less fleshy than it had been once. 'Oh Hugh,' Sheila broke out. 'You're so funny.'

He shrugged, leaned back; the plastic cushion sighed. She wore a dress of patterned red on white, thin shoulder straps, and Fuller was reminded of her deftness. It was her first visit to Africa and she had brought the right things. She was neat and composed; he was soiled and used. He decided not to tell her about Jacob yet.

'What about the Samaritans?'

'I thought I'd let them die for once.' She kept her smile.

'Nuclear disarmament?'

'I'm risking it.'

They fell quiet, Sheila waiting, Fuller lost until he remembered the normal and asked, 'When did you get here? I don't even know how you got here.'

'I just arrived last night. The people here were wonderful. They went out of their way to be nice to me. Everyone seems to know you, Hugh. They were so funny about whether they should put me in your room or not. It seems they have been keeping your room for you for the last two months. They argued among themselves in their own language as if I had nothing to do with it and every now and again one would turn to me and say, "I'm sorry madam," before going back to the argument. I think it had something to do with your girlfriend, Regina. In the end I said I definitely wanted a room of my own because I wanted to sleep. Even then I thought someone was going to insist I should get into your bed whether I liked it or not.'

'I'm pleased you came.'

'You sound surprised.'

'I didn't know.'

'I was getting worried that I would not find you. You know it's silly but it never occurred to me before I left that you might not be easy to find. Kangaba doesn't look very big on the map. When the people here said they didn't know where you were I began to get scared.'

'You always manage well enough without me.'

'No, Hugh! I only manage.' There was vehemence in her voice and Fuller was horrified to see a moisture in her eyes. 'I thought you might not come back this time,' she added quietly, as if ashamed. 'Ted Schwartz in Washington kept phoning me and telling me there was nothing to worry about, but had I heard from you? I started to worry then.' Fuller smiled and Sheila said it was the first time that he had. 'And your letters . . .'

'I'll try and find some coffee, love.'

'Take care Hugh.'

'It's all safe now.'

'I didn't mean that. I don't know what I meant. Of me, I suppose.'

'I'll get the coffee.'

The old man who used to bring Fuller coffee in the mornings was asleep on a grass mat on the kitchen floor. He made a fuss of Fuller who stayed with him – staying away – while he fiddled with the powdered milk, the instant coffee. Over the old man's protests he helped to carry it all into the lounge, the tiny milk jug feeling strange in his village-roughened hand.

'I tried to contact Jacob – you said he was an important man here – but nobody would tell me where he was. In the end I tried the British High Commission and they found you. I was looking forward to seeing Jacob again.'

'I'm afraid Jacob's dead.' He hesitated, then decided. 'A car accident.'

'Oh, I am sorry. Recently?'

'A couple of weeks ago. Before the riots.'

'Did you go to his funeral?'

'No . . . . I didn't know.'

'I liked him. It's so sad.'

'Yes. He was always kind to us.'

They were silent together for a time, then Sheila brightly asked: 'And your girlfriend Regina, how is she?'

'She's OK. She's not in Kingston at the moment.'

'Really, Hugh, a girlfriend. At your age it should at least be a mistress.' She took a breath, then added more quietly, 'Is it serious? Should I have stayed at home?' She bent forward over her coffee and seemed ready to flee inward.

'I don't know. I thought so. We've been close. I'm fond of her. She's been good to me . . . I don't mean you shouldn't have come.'

'I'm just happy that someone has been looking after you,' said Sheila, still studying her coffee. 'I haven't done a very good job of it.'

Fuller looked up at her, astonished.

Regina stood between them, the hem of her out-of-place party dress drooping at the front, her eyebrows high and round. She looked slapped. Fuller let himself be distracted for a moment by the red ankle-strap shoes he had paid for, her toes too calloused for the dainty style. Not speaking, Regina swung both arms, the one with the handbag slapping her dress. Even in her nervousness the movement was easy, as if her long fingers were heavily weighted. She's African, thought Fuller for no good reason, simultaneously setting her aside and prizing her.

'Regina.' He spoke gently and captured one swinging arm by its trinketed wrist, already comforting her for a hurt he had not yet decided to deal her. 'I was not expecting you.'

She looked at him, beginning then discarding an attempt to understand these foolish words. 'This is Sheila?' It was a statement addressed only to Fuller, the last words to be spoken within their intimacy.

'Yes . . . Sheila, I want you to meet Regina. She's my friend, the girl I wrote to you about.' After a moment, out of a desperate fairness, he added, 'Regina, this is Sheila – my wife.'

Sheila formed a smile, went to offer her hand but stayed it at a flicker, leaving it resting on her knee. Regina only looked, big-eyed. 'Please sit with me,' said Sheila, and Regina dropped abruptly on to the sofa, her hands dived between her knees, her expression unchanged. 'I decided to surprise Hugh,' Sheila explained. 'He didn't know I was coming.'

Regina remained looking at Sheila. There was no malice in the look, no more than there would have been in regarding a natural disaster, a fire, a storm, a war. Around her, it seemed to Fuller, hope fell away as he had seen her party dresses slip to the floor.

'I'll get you a Coke,' he offered. 'I saw the barman just go past.'

Ignoring this but looking up into Fuller's face, grey beneath the tan, Regina said, 'She is pretty, your wife. She is not old. She is pretty. Your women do not get old.'

When Fuller found the barman he was talking to two of the girls from reception. They were quietly serious as he reached them but the barman turned to him to ask brightly, 'Your madam has arrived, Mr Fuller?'

'A surprise visit. She decided I could not be trusted on my own. I need looking after.'

The barman nodded; the girls looked past Fuller through the door to where the women sat. Fuller did not follow their stares.

'Can you give me a Coke for Regina?'

'Yes, Mr Fuller. We have saved a few for special occasions. You want me to put some gin in it?'

'Regina doesn't drink gin.'

The barman chuckled, the girls smiled. 'Yes, she drinks it. She likes gin.'

Fuller hesitated. It was as if Regina was already being reclaimed. Or he had never had her. 'Are you sure?'

'Yes, Mr Fuller. Sure.'

'OK, put in some gin. Double.'

'And for madam?'

'The same.'

'No problem. I'll bring it to you. Now I think you'll drink this, Mr Fuller.' He filled a greasy tumbler with whisky. 'I took it out when I saw you with your two wives.'

Sheila and Regina were talking but stopped with Fuller's arrival.

'We were just talking about you,' volunteered Sheila, and Regina grew a slow smile to match her quicker one. Their bare shoulders touched and Fuller remembered each of them: Regina's fine-grained skin, somehow loose-fitting yet exactly right; Sheila's smoothness, the down of tiny fair hairs. 'Regina says she will take me home. You didn't tell me she had children.'

As if this was a cue, Regina stood and Sheila, unsure, stood with her, looking to Fuller, then back to Regina. 'Should we go now?' Regina nodded, yes, assumed her perfect poise.

For a few moments Fuller looked at them, still holding his glass, then smiled and sat. 'I'll see you later.' A new surprise and him still unprepared.

63

How would it be, Fuller asked himself, his spirits rising wildly, if we took Regina back to England? Sheila isn't jealous. They even seem to get on.

He was back in his old seat in the Ambassador lounge, the early evening breeze eddying around him. He had drunk the tumbler of whisky and the two gin and Cokes he ordered for the women. The barman had come by and left the remains of the bottle of whisky on the table with only a smile for comment. He seemed sure that Fuller would not sit there again.

We have the money – that's not a problem. We could set Regina up in a house in Kingston and come and visit her here. And she could visit us in Newbury. The neighbours would be surprised – it would be good for them. There would be plenty of room in the house with the children going away to school and so on. She'd love visiting Oxford Street. He thought of taking Regina shopping, patiently waiting while Regina's uncomplicated pleasure in nice things ran its course. She would be happy. And who knows what she might be capable of if she had the chance of an education. Sheila might like the companionship, the interest – she wouldn't have the children any more. It would be like having two homes instead of one: England and Kangaba. When he travelled he would no longer be a stranger. He would have a place to go, family connections. If he worked he would not be an interfering outsider who belonged nowhere but someone helping his friends and their friends. It would be sane. Summer in Newbury, Regina chic in well-cut dresses. Winter by the Kangaban sea, Sheila brown and busy. It was only a question of being bold, spanning the gap.

He imagined:

'You like Sheila, don't you, Regina?'

'Yes Hoo, I like her.'

'Even though you wanted to be my wife?'

'Sheila is your senior wife.'

'But you can't be my wife as well. You know that.'

'It's all right. I ask Sheila and she says it is all right.'

'To be my wife?'

'To be your family. It's the same thing. Sheila, she understands we African women.'

'She understands?'

'Yes. She is a woman!' He imagined Regina laughing and patting him on his paunch. 'You'll see, it will be good for you. Maybe I'll have a baby for you both.'

64

An ordinary white envelope containing a thousand dollars lay on the table between them. On it was written in pencil – Sheila's hand – Regina's Home Loan. Fuller had placed it there before Regina arrived. She had not touched it.

'Regina, I'm told I have to leave Kangaba today. The Bank has bought my ticket. Sheila is upstairs packing.'

Regina's hands were between her knees. She showed him the ball of tight black curls which was her lowered head. When she raised her eyes it was to dart looks at the inconsequential comings and goings of the reception girls somewhere over Fuller's shoulder.

'Why did you leave Dubeng?' asked Fuller, remembering her straighter back and livelier ways. She shrugged, already seeming to be swallowed by her past, advertising a knowledge of hopelessness she believed Fuller could not possess. He pressed on, denying all this. 'You seemed settled when I left. They liked having you there.'

She pulled her dress down over her knees, smoothed it needlessly. She craned to watch an incident by the door. She sighed. She squashed her lips together, pushed them ruefully askew – not without charm. Fuller waited. The plane was already at the airport.

She spoke very softly, so he had to lean towards her. 'Was not the same after you were gone. I – I . . . it was different on my own . . . They are not my people.' She paused then let herself become more fluent. 'The Alkalo comes to me and says I am not to keep our house. He says it was promised to his son when he marries and I cannot keep it. He says it was alright when I was with you but now I am on my own it is not alright. I tell him you are coming back and he does not know what to say. The women try to support me but they can do nothing against the men. Then the Alkalo, he comes to our house with the koranic teacher and they tell me that I am in a Moslem village and I have to obey Moslem ways. I say, what are those Moslem ways? and he tells me that it is not right for a single woman of my age to live on her own. I must belong to a man's family. He says that if you do not come back he will make me his fourth wife. I laugh and he gets angry at me and tells me I am too proud. I know he is jealous of our house, that is why he wants me to leave. I say to him, if this is such a good Moslem village, how is it that they drink palm wine? Then I say again that you are coming back and he should be very careful. I look for you these days.

'After three days he comes to me again and says he knows you are not coming back to Dubeng. I tell him he is wrong but I know he is telling the truth. Later, in the night, he comes to me in our house. He force me. I could not resist him. I – I have no brothers in that village. Early in the morning I packed what I could carry on my head and walked to the town. Some of the women help me get away. I took the first lorry to Kingston. It was a terrible journey – three days. So many check-points. The SDF thugs just thieved everybody's belongings.' She paused a moment. 'I think the women in Dubeng will regret me.'

'I'm sorry . . . They arrested me. Sort of . . . Kamara is out of the country.'

Regina nodded, shrugged and nodded again to neutralise the shrug. Then she looked direct at Fuller, her brows intense, her voice urgent. 'Hoo, I loves you! I loves you, Hoo!' There was more impatience than anger – frustration that this man could not see the obvious but wilfully concealed the simple under the complex, failing, in the end, to see through the differences to an equality of love.

Fuller slumped back in his seat, his throat choked, hating this, his heart flooding out. He knew what he would do and was grateful that it was to the top of her head and not to her eyes that he now spoke. 'Maybe,' he said, words treacherous enough to slash her love, 'maybe I'll be back one day.'

They sat silent and immobile for a long time. At last it was Fuller who knew he had to go. He stood, touched her on her slender neck with his big, rough hand. She did not respond. He pushed the envelope closer and said quietly, 'This is for you.' He walked away to the stairs which led to the room where Sheila packed his bag, but waited long enough to see that Regina reached out for the envelope and held it in her hand.

In Libya Kamara had been pleading for guns. A fat, alcoholic diplomat had promised help in the days before Uncle threw the Libyans out, and two of Kamara's friends had gone to train in Tripoli, where their blackness won them harsh treatment.

News of the riots, the failed revolt, came to Kamara in the night. Five soldiers called him and the other Kangabans from the hostel and wordlessly cuffed them around their heads. Kamara argued noisily but they cuffed him hardest until his ears rang and he stood silent. It was not through English or any of the five Kangaban languages he spoke fluently that Kamara learned of the premature and bungled uprising, but through the barely recollected Arabic of childhood koranic school. The Libyans were displeased; the Kangabans were fools; their fate would be decided; it was now of little consequence. When the Libyans had tired and their anger cooled Kamara dared to ask about the dead. Maybe a thousand, the soldier thought, maybe two. Who knows?

A few hours later, with the dawn, Kamara slipped away from the hostel on his own and was in the centre of Tripoli by the time the airline office opened. Strictly speaking it was not permitted, but Kamara, through the trick of charm and confidence, was able to exchange his return ticket to Kangaba for a ticket to London on a plane leaving in the afternoon. At Tripoli International he expected to be stopped but, although there were men in dark glasses and they may have been watching him, there was no move and he left uncertain whether his departure had been desired or simply overlooked.

The immigration official at Heathrow looked at Kamara's red Kangaban passport, looked at Kamara.

233

'Holiday,' offered Kamara as reason for his visit.

'No,' replied the official. Where was his return ticket to Kangaba? He would have to wait.

In a bare room, not yet in the United Kingdom, Kamara was told that he was trying it on; he certainly was not wanted. He must return to Libya or, failing that, Kangaba. He could not stay. There was no choice.

He was left for four hours before two more officials arrived, a woman in uniform and a man in a suit. The woman demanded, with a simple confidence, all the papers from his pockets and his bag. While the man asked questions about Kamara's future and his past, the woman noted down addresses on a clipboard.

When they had finished the man looked at his watch. 'There's a plane to Kingston in an hour. We are going to put you on it.' The voice was soft and unassertive, as if his right to dispose of Kamara had been long agreed between them.

Kamara replied, now earnest, sweat now breaking out on his forehead, that he would be returning to his certain death.

'You should have thought of that.'

'This is not justice. I am a member of the British Commonwealth. I have the right to be a political refugee. I have friends. There will be a big scandal. I can guarantee you that!'

The official nodded. 'The policeman will escort you to the plane.'

The time for the Kingston plane passed. An older man, more rumpled, put his head round the door, raised his eyebrows at finding Kamara alone. 'Mr Kamara?'

'Yes.'

'You'd better come to my office.'

This office was used. There was a desk crowded with papers, a wall of files, a potted plant. A young woman brought in two cups of coffee in mugs and placed one in front of Kamara.

'So, where would you stay if we let you in? Who are your friends?' The man leaned back in his swivel chair.

No, the names and addresses of Kangaban students would not

do, so Kamara came to Fuller. Hugh Fuller, Kamara said, was his close friend. They had worked together in Kangaba, he was an important man, had been a professor at Oxford University, had worked for this and that international organisation. He lived in a place called Newbury. Mr Fuller would certainly vouch for Kamara and offer him a place to stay. Except it is possible he might still be in Kangaba.

'Stay here.' He wrinkled a conspiratorial smile at Kamara. 'I'll only be a minute.'

It had been dark for hours; the clock read eleven. This was the day that started with the Libyan soldiers, Kamara reminded himself.

'We'll phone,' the official said when he returned. His voice was low and he brought a chair next to Kamara's on the wrong side of the desk. He dialled and then, in a polite, clear voice, asked to speak to Mr Fuller.

Months later Kamara was to tell Sheila's mother during his single visit to Newbury – charming the old lady in spite of his blackness – that he could clearly hear her voice while she talked to the immigration official. It was the high cracked voice of a genteel old lady born before telephones and who still imagined you had to shout. Her tone was alarmed. Probably it was after her bedtime. Oh dear, no, Mr Fuller was not there, nor was Sheila, his wife, her daughter. They were still both in Kangaba. She was just looking after the house, you see. Oh no, she couldn't imagine how to contact them in Kangaba. Through Hugh's work perhaps. Did she know of a friend of Hugh's, a Mr Kamara from Kangaba? Goodness me, no, she didn't know, but – yes – there had been something in a letter, she thought that was the name, something African anyway – she was an old lady. She didn't understand Hugh's work but, yes, it was true he's an international expert, quite an important man. And, yes, she expected him home very soon, or at least Sheila.

Kamara was admitted to the United Kingdom seven hours later, in time to catch an early morning tube. He had looked for buses but had quickly become confused and colder than he had ever known. An Australian girl waiting out the night in Terminal Three had finally explained to him how to find his way to Bayswater. He would remember her friendliness and ease.

The basement in a part of Bayswater which had not yet become fashionable was shared by a shifting population of Kangaban students who declared a common belief that if they returned Uncle would kill them for their politics. They passed on to Kamara a thick winter coat which, although he often wore it over his bare skin, failed to meet across his chest – a chest made broad for an event he missed. In the mornings, in his coat, Kamara walked to Queensway and lingered over coffee in the window of a fast food restaurant. For the first few days he read *The Times*, because he had heard of it, but Kangaba was only mentioned once and after that he read the *Sun* because the other Africans did. There were not, he noted, any scandal-sheets in London. The people were kept in the dark.

Only the BBC World Service seemed to remember Kangaba. It reported that all was quiet, order had been restored, the widespread looting had died down. 'It looks as if,' Our Own Correspondent observed, 'the government of President Funna – or Uncle as he is universally known in Kangaba – has ridden out the latest crisis and won itself a further term in power. For the time being at least, he has managed to draw together the support, which includes Kangaba's powerful Lebanese business community, to continue in office. But while the President's political skills have been very much in evidence during the recent food riots, it has to be said that he is now a very old man and most observers believe that as long as the underlying problems of poverty and corruption remain unaddressed further crises will be unavoidable. Perhaps next time the opposition will be better organised and have stronger allies. It is this prospect which has sent the Western powers and the international financial organisations scurrying to put together a rescue package of loans to bail out the beleaguered Kangaban economy. The task is not made easier by the death of Dr Jacob Cesay, the dapper, Oxford-educated Minister for Economic Affairs who, so far, is the only senior politician to be implicated in the bungled coup attempt.

'While Kingston breathes a sigh of relief and gets back to business as normal, there remains an uneasiness within the diplomatic community about President Funna's style of government. Many consider that the days of his sort of old-fashioned, idiosyncratic African leadership are numbered and will not be missed. But, as one Western diplomat I talked to put it: "He has his faults but at least when Uncle talks to us we know he talks for Kangaba." What he meant, of course, was that he doesn't talk for Moscow.'

Kamara walked in the rain very fast. In London you could not just move around; no one talked in the street, there was no one to visit. The other Kangabans in the basement where he was suffered as a guest, were fakes, their political pretensions false. The London rain sluiced across the pavements of Westbourne Grove and was disposed of down drains as easily and discreetly as news from Kangaba. Water trickled down his neck, he pressed his thin-soled shoes against the paving stones, daring them to slip. He wore no hat and the rain on his face could not have been distinguished from tears or perspiration. All was quiet in Kangaba, the looting had died down. A thousand dead, maybe two, who knows? He only knew for sure that he was not among them.

In Queensway, suited Middle-Easterners stood under black umbrellas waiting for their cars. Teenage German tourists in pastel clothes darted from awning to awning like hunters. Kamara, strong and wet, strode through them, brushing shoulders, but no one wanted to fight him.

After Queensway the Bayswater Road was unpopulated and bleak under the high lights and evening wet. The cars moved fast, trailing spray. To his left the buildings were high and set back from the road, twice diminishing him, once by size and once by affluence. On his right Hyde Park was black and lush behind its railings.

Half-way to Marble Arch, half-way across the road, Kamara, half-running, came to a sudden halt, clinging dizzily to a traffic island, suddenly unconvinced that his forward progress compensated for the absence of a destination. Cars passed on both sides, adding grime to the sodden flared jeans – unfashionable in London – clinging to his calves. He turned to follow with his eyes the tail-lights of a car on its way towards Holland Park and tried by an act of pure will to imagine its destination, the place of the driver in the world's design. He could not. He turned again, searching after a car heading towards the West End. And again he turned, his eyes stamped with the sight of a man reclined in the corner of a limousine's back seat, reading documents by a yellow light. It could have been the man who decided about Kangaba. He was suddenly convinced it was and looked after the car long after it had disappeared, ignoring all others. 'I have to learn all this,' he told himself, calmed by the discovery of a task. 'It was not enough to know Kangaba. I have to learn all this.'